Sessions

with a

Demon

Ren will make you laugh!

Best wishes
will suit
for long!

[signature]

Sessions with a Demon

FINN O'MALLEY

Cover design by Jayelle at Dream Saver Covers
Photo by Transparency with Meagan
Edited by Andrea Coble at Daresay Editing

ISBN: 978-1-7341135-0-1

Library of Congress Control Number: 2019915613

For Caleb

Sometimes silly ideas become a catalyst, changing our direction in a moment, hurling us toward the dreams we didn't realize were possible.

We alone hold the choice in how we respond to the chaos that is our lives.

PROLOGUE

The twinge of paranoia tracing over your skin that sends you racing up a dark set of stairs. Gooseflesh bursting from your skin for no apparent reason, making your heart skip a beat, leaving you on edge. A torment of fear settling into your mind, rooting into the murkiest places, making you feel despondent and isolated within the confines of your thoughts.

All of these things are me.

You don't see me, but I am there, gnawing at the edges of your vision, the shimmer in the corner of your eye.

I am what terrifies you most. I can change your life in a second, have you begging, pleading for mercy, and praying to a god you aren't even sure you believe in.

My purpose is to leave you scattered, misguided, and separated from your authentic self. My process is slow and methodical, all to keep you under my control, bending your will at my command.

I am a Synergy Demon.

But my boss has a new health care plan and now I have new therapist.

CHAPTER ONE
My Complaints

My thumb rubbed the woven thread of the couch, worn thin by the hundreds of lost souls who sat here before me. Tiny chevron stripes stared back, dizzying me into a mere depression by their ugly nature.

I don't belong here.

Shifting my robes, I pulled my ankle over my knee, leaning back into a loose spring, the padding long lost to the heavy bodies of its prior occupants.

Apparently, our health plan must be a cheap one.

I stared at Dr. Lilith Madson.

"I'm glad you are here, Ren." Her voice was soothing, like fingertips delicately sliding over satin. I only grunted my answer.

"Your . . . plan . . . requires you to be present once a week as part of your current assignment, is that correct?" The doctor peered at the notepad resting in her lap.

"My assignment? That's what we're going to call her?" I asked, tugging my robes again, my pale sinewy fingers in sharp contrast to the dark velvet.

In response to my tone, a perfectly shaped eyebrow raised above thick black framed glasses, and subtle wrinkles flooded her forehead.

"She is a menace."

"A menace? Hardly, Ren, she's a mere human." Her pen tapped the notepad in a sporadic up and down motion.

My eyebrows shot up. "Have you met her?"

"I received her file and did a complete follow through of my own. I understand why you are struggling." Her hands touched at the edge of the notepad.

I shadowed Dr. Madson, a well-known Demon therapist, for several weeks before agreeing to meet with her. She held traditional titles, and degrees from the earth realm as well as several higher certificates from the Realm of Hidden Shadows.

"Couldn't you glamor a more inviting office?" My eyes questioned as I inferred the dimly lit room and lousy sofa beneath me, while her luxurious leather chair, the color of melted butter, didn't go unnoticed.

"Does it matter to you, the aesthetics of our visits?" The doctor's eyes narrowed. I would march straight to the doors of Heaven before I would allow her to analyze me.

"She has cats." My mouth twisted into a pout.

"Lots of humans own cats, Ren." The pen danced in her hand again. "Even Demons have been known to keep cats."

"Three, to be precise." I pushed sweaty palms over the thick velvet. "Simon, Beelzebub, let me tell you how offensive *that* is, and Cupcake. Who names a cat Cupcake? The cat hates it by the way. Of course, my *assignment* would never think to ask." I did ask, and the long-haired orange and white fur-face ridiculed her owner. As punishment, Cupcake brought her dead birds every Tuesday. I admired Cupcake, poor cat.

Dr. Madson scribbled notes across the heavy paper. What was it about therapists who had you word vomiting before you realized what you were doing? Though I was well aware of the doctor's affluent abilities, I hadn't realized how keen she would be.

"What about the cats bothers you?" Madson glanced up from the paper.

My hand met my mouth, tracing my bottom lip before speaking again, stubble nipping my delicate skin. "Do you know how long it takes to repair these robes? Simon made it his personal mission to shred every spell I weave into the fibers. The last time I had to wait four days before the material would hold a spell, and Simon glared at me for an entire week with absolute cat satisfaction."

"Certainly, you have spare robes?" Dr. Madson pushed her glasses up on her nose.

"Certainly, that isn't the point." The edge of my teeth grabbed the tip of my thumb.

"And what about Karen?"

And there it was, finally, the doctor reached her modus operandi. Karen. My *assignment*. My inhale was almost as sharp as my exhale. Where to begin? Debating internally, I tapped my lips. Karen had become a problem. Thousands of years of demonic haunting and Karen, a five-five lippy excuse for a human, forced me to contemplate the meaning of my very existence.

"She is . . . complicated." My delay in responding was noted as she scribbled.

"Would you like to elaborate?" The pen waved again, tapping in a rhythmic movement that gnawed on my nerves.

No. I would not like to elaborate, doctor.

"She sages."

"Sages? The new-agey concept of wafting around smoke to dematerialize evil and negativity?" A Cheshire smile bloomed across her mouth, followed by a sinister bark of laughter. "Those humans do make me laugh."

"Aren't you part human?"

"Ren, the human part of me died long ago."

Interesting. I checked the appropriate boxes I had created for the doctor in my mind. I wondered indeed how influenced she might have been for our side. Without hesitation I weaved a few protection spells for my thoughts. I didn't need her digging around where she

7

didn't belong. One would have thought this would be a violation of privacy, but the machinations of the demonic never ceased to amaze me. Although she herself wasn't demonic, my employer, on the other hand, was, and always would be.

"Why do you think your usual techniques aren't working on Karen?" Her writing hand waited.

"Maybe she is impervious to my skills, as grand as they are. Perhaps she is protected by him and his hoity-toity angels. I don't know. If I knew…" The good doctor grated on me, creating creases of anxiety on my forehead, in my semi-physical form.

"I see." Her hands folded across the paper, encapsulating the pen. I wanted to rip the pen out of her slim fingers and chuck it into another dimension. Instead, taking a breath, I rested my head on my fist, the scratchy material of the couch chaffing my elbow.

"Why do you think she elicits such a response?"

Images of throttling the doctor, along with her incessant questions, played out in my mind. Such a *human* reaction. One which often occurred in Karen's presence as well. Ripples teased through my subconscious, the ramblings of something I'd read somewhere. The feeling tugged the dark recesses of my training from long ago. I refocused back on the doctor.

"Perhaps this is a test, a difficult assignment to assess my abilities," I offered, shifting my body against the horrid sofa.

"Is that what you feel like this is? A test?" Her sparkling blue eyes pierced my magic.

Well, well, doctor.

Her presence subtle, like the sun on a cool morning, I permitted her invasive search through my shimmers, allowing her to see only what I deemed necessary. Whose side was she on? Mine or my boss? The questions lingered in my mind as my eyes narrowed, ending her exploration.

"Find what you were looking for?"

"What?" The doctor stuttered. "I am sorry. Part of my clinical duty is to check for any malignancies. Something you aren't aware of." She shifted in the chair, a slender finger scratching the back of her neck. "I apologize for the intrusion."

I waved off her devious examination.

"Test or not, you will need to accomplish your work with Karen."

As if I don't know this already.

"Have you mapped her soul weaknesses? Gone through her darkest moments? Perhaps you missed something." Her body pulled forward toward me, leaning over her notebook.

My eyebrows twitched downward, irritation scratching at the surface of my skin. Asking me if I properly studied my assignment, alluding that I, a Synergy Demon, missed something with the skill set I developed for the demons directly beneath me, rattled something inside of me.

I moved my legs again, jaw jutting out in defiance. "As much as this is to my annoyance, she is genuinely a decent person." The words held a slight edge I hadn't intended.

"Impossible." The doctor snarked. "All humans are weak. You must find the precise place to puncture their core and permeate until you create a cesspool of frailty. Then you repeat and reopen the wound until the shatter is complete."

The words hung stagnant between us. Shock rippled over me, not at her words, they were standard protocol, after all, but the vehemence with which she enjoyed them. My hand drug through my hair in a swift motion as I considered her and the darkness looming behind those startling eyes. If the doctor's level of evil concerned me, maybe I was off my game. Perhaps something was indeed amiss.

I am the demon here.

Synergy demons had been created to synergistically work with humans to create an exchange of energy through negative-impact emotions. This was my livelihood, how I survived for thousands of years. If the doctor thought I was unable to correctly exchange energy, to feed off humans, what would happen? I pushed the thoughts aside.

"I will take some time to re-evaluate her and my techniques," I extended in compliance. However, I would be evaluating more than just Karen. The doctor inspired a new fascination, something sinister lurking in the crevices, intriguing me to dig deeper.

"Well, let's leave the session here. In a week we will discuss your findings." Dr. Madson's petunia-pink lips turned upward into a smile. I nodded as I vanished from the dingy office hoping the next session would bring a better couch.

With my evilness in question, I reappeared in Karen's home, sliding through an opening unnoticed during her last sage-fest. The majority of humans didn't pay attention to such things and we were diligently trained to find the crevices and barge through.

Beelzebub, the Russian Blue, laid sprawled across the middle of the living room floor, legs stretched across the sunlight patches on the carpet. At my entrance his ears twitched, glaring yellow eyes watching me as I shifted into my slinky, shadowed form. Without hesitation the cat smacked his paw with a quick *bap-bap-bap* at the dark tendrils cascading around him before hissing and tearing out of the room.

"Not so nice after all." I muttered to the empty room.

CHAPTER TWO
Troublesome Thoughts

I spent my week following Lilith. The doctor led quite the interesting life, moving in and out of the realms. Several of my underlings met with her for long sessions and I questioned what she had in store for them. The sudden need for therapy amongst my kind was slightly concerning.

Dr. Madson changed the location of our session from the shitty couch in Lexington, Kentucky to New York, New York. Hope surged in the back of my mind for a posh chair.

Pondering these thoughts, and my next session, I walked the busy streets of Manhattan amongst the preoccupied humans. Something about leering next to them as they sauntered through their day completely unaware of our existence brought a smile to my lips. Humans always joked about teleportation and how amazing it would be, but the odd thing? I actually missed walking at times. A struggle they would never understand.

"Hey, what do you think you're doing?"

My head jerked upward at the question directed at me by a female voice.

"Yea, you, buddy." My progress halted, her hazel-blue eyes met mine as arms wrapped in soft worn leather folded across her chest.

Glancing around, I tried to find the person she spoke to, as it clearly couldn't be me. Humans were unable to see those of us who dwell in the ethereal.

"What are you doing down here, walking like you belong with them?" Her foot tapped in sporadic movement and the cords to her ear buds swayed in unison.

"Are you speaking to me?" My normally throaty voice felt indistinct to my ears.

"Who the hell else would I be yelling at in the middle of the sidewalk?" Her lips twitched with annoyance, and her thoughts came barreling through my mind.

She thinks I'm an idiot.

"Believe me, I don't particularly like to pretend I am on the phone, yelling at some other person. It's a pain in the ass."

What in the devil? I considered the petite woman. My eyes tightened, still perplexed by her awareness of me.

"You guys are all the same. Stunned and shocked someone can freaking see you." Sarcastically feigning shock, her body tilted before she abruptly about-faced, walking away.

Feet locked in place, I gawked awkwardly.

"Well, are you coming or not?" She called over her shoulder.

A horn blaring to my left startled me into forward motion and I followed the long bob of dark hair weaving around the other humans.

"You can see me." An uneven statement rather than a question.

"Of course I can." At the stoplight she stopped, waiting with the mass of people for the little white walking man to glow again. "My question still stands, what are you doing down here? And in this form?"

Direct questions rolling from her small mouth made me look down at my human shape. In this form I appeared human-like, but trails of shadows ribboned around me, alluding to my supernatural essence. A corporeal body was entirely different, which was required if I wanted to interact on a human level, as one of them. It was rarely done, if ever, because of the impact on our ethereal bodies. So, the question begged, how did the human know of my presence, and to the degree of being capable of speaking to me?

"You're a Synergy Demon, aren't you?" She moved forward with the crowd of people traveling as a swarm across the street. "Aren't you supposed to be lurking about in the dark recesses of their minds instead of out here waltzing around?" She waved her hand in a swirling movement, encompassing the chaos of people around her.

I had to quicken my steps to catch up with her. "How do you know what I am?" Perplexed by her knowledge, I stopped at one question before the barreling of others began.

"Pssshh. I know all about you nut-sacks and your devious, bullshit scams to ruin our lives." Her face turned toward me in a sharp motion, eyes boring into mine.

Her words assaulted me in ways I didn't expect, shame rippling in uncomfortable waves. The beautiful dance of our slow decimation of souls, sliced into crass accusation left pin pricks of compunction.

Fury followed.

"Who do you think you are?" I grabbed her arm, ignoring the penetrating shocks radiating through my hand. Touching a human required preparation, to block their soul light before it damaged the soulless black of a demon's essence.

Her small body whipped around by my quick movements more than I intended. Humans were delicate, fragile creatures, which is the reason physical contact is generally not permitted.

Anger slashed through her hazel eyes as she yanked her arm from my grip. "You do not touch me. Ever." Her words snapped in a staccato rhythm. "You have no idea what you're a part of." She absently rubbed her arm where I had grabbed.

My teeth grated against each other as I contemplated what she said. What did she mean? Something about her scratched my curiosity.

Before I could ask, she darted off into the thick crowd of people. Bodies brushed against me, bumping and nudging to get by as I tracked her movements. An icy glare narrowed on me before she disappeared down the stairs to the subway.

The bizarre encounter left me irked. Thoughtfully, I checked the time, finding I was late for my appointment. In a quick shimmer I left my human form in exchange for dark shadows and vanished from the street.

My knuckles rapped against the sleek modern door before entering. A classy office, bright with natural light from long wide windows revealed the New York skyline. Stark white couches stood out against the deep gray carpet. I found Lilith waiting behind a desk. A blond crown of curls bounced as she nodded, glancing up from her computer.

"Ah, Ren. Good to see you." She shifted herself around the desk to sit on the couch opposite me.

"And you." I said. The sofa enveloped me in soft leather, plush and comfortable. "Now, *this* is a glamor."

Head tilting with a small smile, she met my gaze. "I'm glad you're comfortable."

I watched her settle in, as she tucked one leg under the other, I realized she intentionally made me uncomfortable last time. I pondered her intentions.

"How did your week go with Karen? Did you make any progress?" She rested her hands on the knees of her black dress slacks.

Today's session didn't include the notebook, and thank Hell below, the annoying pen.

My hand drug across the bottom of my chin. *Karen.*

"I believe I have a new direction to move with her." I lied. Well. Sort of. Karen currently in the *off* status with her boyfriend created a slow slide into a self-loathing pity party, which made my job much easier. However, I hadn't bothered with her much, having been so preoccupied by Lilith and her odd obsessive behavior.

"That is wonderful, Ren. See, a little backtracking is sometimes necessary." Her eyes glittered.

I tuned out the rest of her ramblings as my mind jumped to the mysterious girl on the street. I did not find a trace of magic within her, but the mental projection shields had been obvious. Without thinking, I tried searching for her, a subtle scan of the souls in the vicinity. A perk of the job, to instantly find certain soul signatures. I came up blank.

"Ren? Did you hear me?" The doctor's eyebrows melded toward each other.

"Yes. Yes. Using her current depression to seize opportunity." Another perk-- being able to replay the conversation so I didn't miss anything. My response merited another cheerful smile.

"She could be a valuable asset to your committee."

"Who?" I asked, thinking only of Hazel-eyes.

"Karen!"

An edge to Lilith's voice pulled me into the present.

"Yes, of course. The meeting yesterday demonstrated the value of these current acquisitions." My words dragged off again as I wondered how I would find *her*.

"You seem distracted today, is something else bothering you?" Lips pursed, she crossed her arms, drawing my attention to the vibrant red top she wore. Sharply contrasting the entire room, it burned my eyes, like some sort of prophetic beacon screaming in a language I didn't understand.

"Just the cats. Karen made a cake to celebrate Cupcake's fourth birthday. She didn't even care to make it cat-edible, just a damn cake for herself." I ranted. Really, I didn't care about the cake, although I did find it offensive. She didn't offer the fluff of orange and white some kind of treat. But the doctor did seem weirdly obsessed with Karen.

"Selfishness is an excellent behavior to feed. This is fantastic work, Ren." She leaned back into the leather, checking the time on her smart watch. "Her ego is key to creating the energy we desire."

My head ticked at her use of the word *we*. Which *we* did she mean, precisely?

"Yes, I have created several cords of discontentment, severed her grounding cord to create a lack of connection, which is slowly detaching her from self. Things should move more quickly now." Substantiating my processes with the doctor would get old, if this was what she expected, but for the time being I tried to placate.

"Very good." Blue eyes shimmered. "Do you think you can begin the acquisition soon?"

My eyes shot from the window to the doctor. "I thought we wanted their vibration as low as possible first?"

Lilith's head gave a small nod and her lips tightened. "You're right. We wouldn't want to rush the process." She smoothed her pants with her hands, picking off a small piece of lint and tossing it aside.

But under her cool exterior she did want to rush, an antsy stream running through her energy, barely detectable. The doctor had nothing to do with our work, not directly, and especially not the outcome. However, something in her eyes struck me, a quick flash, leaving me curious. With canny efficiency, I pushed through her auric field, into thick trails of heavy dense energy.

"No, Crastin wants these souls to be the best possible sources," I said, referring to my boss and upper-level demon. While distracting her with my words, I continued my search. A treacherous maze of intentionally layered walls impeded my progress. Dr. Madson was hiding something, but I would need to finish my search of her emotional soul map later.

I desperately wanted to know what required an intricate labyrinth of magical protections.

CHAPTER THREE
Problems

Heavy beads of water rushed down the thick glass as the misty clouds sunk deeper into the city, reminding everyone the storm's wrath hadn't finished yet. The fourth consistent day of rain edged on, and prickled, my already foul mood. Hazel-eyes troubled me for the past two weeks, provoking fruitless searches through New York. She vanished, like some cruel joke to my abilities, remaining a complete mystery. And it was as irritating as Heaven above.

Until the day she popped up on my radar.

A crack of thunder reverberated throughout the old building, sending a draft over my tendrils. *She just came in here, now where the hell did she go?* I continued to search in shadowed obscurity through the abandoned rooms and hallways laid out before me.

Dr. Madson had been frustrated with me last week at our appointment in Belize. I'm not sure she intended to reveal her emotions, but they were rather obvious. She also backed off in her obsessive questioning about Karen and appeared more like a normal therapist. She found me too distracted, and over what? I refused to answer or tell her that some twenty-something human got the best of me. Or how much it angered me. Which led me to the realization that I was terrible at therapy.

A creak down the hall to the right sent me spinning on the spot, reappearing where the sound had occurred. Silence met my ears and I found another bare room. Unable to feel her energy signature, I debated on ending my hunt yet again. Clenched fists burning under my robes, frustration built like an untamed fire as the emptiness of the area mocked me. Lightning flashed, sending fragments of blue illuminating the barren walls.

What in Lucifer's name was that?

Handwriting, maps, timelines, and a myriad of notes strewn across the walls appeared for the shortest second, and then, darkness. Streaming across the room I dragged my hand over the peeling dingy, gray paint, revealing a thick layer of dust. The mysterious images and writing absent.

"Why are you following me?"

I immediately recognized Hazel-eyes' voice and took my time turning around to face her, meeting her stubborn glare.

"I asked you a question, *demon*." She pushed wet strands of hair off her face.

"I have a name, *human*." I let the hood of my cloak fall back to reveal my face. Her head flinched back the slightest degree, and she crossed her arms in defense.

"It's a sick joke from the Fates' that you are not as hideous as the things you do." The muscles in her jaw twitched wildly as disgust swirled through her energy.

"How are you hiding your demented wall-writing obsession?" My thumb jerked back, gesturing at the invisible psychosis behind me.

The girl's tongue poked into the side of her

cheek as she debated, shifting her weight. "Invisible paint, they sell it at the local hardware store, asshole."

My lip twitched. "Why do you hate me so much?"

"I hate your kind. You know, evil?" A chunky boot tapped the rotting wood floor.

"My name is Ren." For the life of me, I don't know why I shared my name.

"Good, now I know how to identify you when I do a banishment spell." Her lips tugged upward in a sneer.

"Magic, interesting." But her essence felt so *human.* How was she managing to hide everything? Questions toppled over one another as she eyed me. And with another ear-splitting boom, thunder roared, and shards of light unveiled her psychotic, stalker writings.

Because I expected the illumination, I used my abilities to gaze back through the images, and discovered her maniac scribbles weren't simply one wall, but perhaps the entire building. Behind her writing consumed every flat surface and a litany of lists glowed in an iridescent blue sheen. Names of demons who worked for me, who I worked *for*, and circled three times with crazed fervency was Dr. Lilith Madson.

Walking around Hazel-eyes, I stared at the wall behind her. Although I could no longer see the images hidden behind magic, I touched where the doctor's name had been hastily written.

"Who are you?" I gave a half glance over my shoulder.

"What are you planning with Dr. Soul Sucker?" The vehemence in her voice ripped through the room.

"Planning?" I spun to face her. Planning? I was in therapy for Hell's sake. Yes, Dr. Madson, helped to fulfill our duties as demons, lowering vibrations to utilize soul essence light, falling under standard protocol. The core system of two opposing sides, a proverbial tug of war, occurring for centuries. But I wasn't planning anything *with* her. That was absurd.

"You really are clueless, aren't you?" She stepped forward, pity dragging through her facial expressions.

My eyes narrowed, seeking anything in her aura to provide answers. Instead, words tumbled out of my mouth. "Dr. Madson is a therapist. Soul Sucker might be taking things a bit far." Defending the doctor? What was happening? Everything felt off-kilter, reversed, as if my own techniques were being projected back to me. "What are you doing?"

I sensed the magic then, the spell she created to mirror my persuasive synergistic abilities, using them against me. My mouth pulled together, irritation grating my scowl, before admiration struck. Hazel-eyes was intelligent.

She huffed a snort. "Clueless and slow." Her shoulders shifted in her leather jacket. "Are you working on her project?"

Not accustomed to being interrogated by a human, her questions prickled my annoyance. "Why are you obsessed with her?" My eyebrows raised as I indicated the crazy drawn over every surface.

Hazel-eyes considered me for several moments as the wind and rain hammered the window. "She is plotting something."

"Something?" I prodded. "Sounds ominous." Stomaching the chuckle rising in my throat, I regarded the small human before me and wondered what happened to create such zealous behavior.

"I am going to stop her." Lightning radiated the dark sky, highlighting her scribbles, emphasizing her determination.

"Quite gallant of you, however, I doubt you're capable." I circled behind her, forcing her to move. She didn't dare leave her back to me. "Are you going to tell me your name?"

"Why should I give you such power?" Her head tilted. "People rarely realize how much power is in a name."

"How did *you* come to such knowledge?" My body language mirrored hers.

"You are impossible." She groaned and it filled the room. "What are you going to do to Karen?"

"My assignment? How do you know about her?" Hazel-eyes' keen awareness and knowledge began to trouble me.

"Alright, dammit. I can't take any more of this bullshit banter. Dr. Soul Sucker is killing people for their soul light. How you don't know this blows my mind." Her hands mimicked a bomb exploding at her head.

Surprise sent my head jerking back. Killing defeated our goals. We needed souls alive. Distraught, broken and untethered, yes, but not dead. Dead didn't allow for light to slowly be siphoned over years of time.

Dr. Madson wouldn't kill humans, would she? In my mind I flew through my interactions and observances with the doctor. The layered magical protections blanketing her energy, in combination with my intrigue and curiosities driving me to follow her after our appointments led me to believe she was up to something. Teeth nipping down on my lip, I considered the vast scribblings of Hazel-eyes.

"And you came across this information, how?" I edged closer, investigating her energy for lies.

"None of your business," she said through gritted teeth, straightening her spine to increase her height a fraction of an inch.

The energetic truth I sensed in her allegations slammed through me. The doctor's secrets spilling out like unraveling thread. The more I explored Hazel-eyes soul, blockages and walls ascended around her. A traumatic event rippled in the depths of her soul. An oozing flare of anger and guilt roared inside, wrapped tightly around one theme.

Revenge.

How fascinating.

The girl captivated me. Her energy swirled and tilted in places I had never experienced before. Her vengeance was driven by a filtered light, a place of goodness, nestled in the brambles of negative emotions.

Wouldn't that be amusing to interact with?

"I will help you," I said, finishing my examination of her essence.

"You?" Her voice hitched higher, followed by a scoff. "Why would you help me? You don't even know my plan."

"Your plan is simple." With prepared foresight, I cupped her chin with my finger. "Revenge is one of the darkest schemes available to humans. I'm intrigued."

Her jaw jutted out, contemplating my offer. "I'm Ash." She pulled her chin away from my touch.

Finally, Hazel-eyes had a name.

CHAPTER FOUR
Reality

Leaving Ash to her scheming, I focused my attention on Lilith. I didn't disbelieve Ash's conspiracies, but they didn't earn my full faith either. It was difficult to believe the famed demon therapist would actually resort to murdering humans. The doctor arranged this week's session on a private beach in Maui. I found her sitting under an umbrella, normal glasses exchanged for over-sized, dark sunglasses.

"Ah, Ren, glad you're here." A smile melted across her face as she stretched back, putting her feet up on the chair across from her. "Would you like a drink?" She waved her hand in the air gesturing to the man behind the small bar.

I nodded. "Serene location," I said, peering out to the open vast of deep blue water before sitting.

"One of my favorites, and it's a day for celebrating." Her lips, a luscious red, turned upward in a slight smirk.

"Oh?" The warm breeze sent palm fronds swaying against each other as I glanced back at the doctor.

"Oh, yes Ren. The acquisitions have begun. Crastin is extremely pleased." Satisfaction glowed in subtle waves around Lilith.

"Karen is almost ready." The waiter handed me a drink, a slush of yellow, and I tipped it in her direction, showing my gratitude. The sharp tang of tequila sparked as I swallowed.

"That is wonderful news, Ren. Do you feel you have resolved your issues with her?"

I studied her a moment, careful to answer, wishing I could see her soulless eyes. "Mostly. Perhaps sometimes we need a reminder we are not invincible to human minds."

Her laughter shrilled through the air. "Isn't that the truth?" She extended her arm across the table, touching my arm. A reverberation tingled into my bones. I felt her excitement, a lightness, and a thrumming steadily underneath. Both sang of something different. Power.

As palpable as the dense humid air around me, the seeping thread of human energy emanated in vibrant undulations. Though distinctly *not* the doctor's essence, it melded into her, woven into Lilith's essence in a delicate manner, barely detectable at first, but it soon became obvious and disjointed as her hand stayed on my arm.

Ash's accusations of the doctor assaulted me. Killing humans was one thing, wearing their energy like a Dalmatian coat in some sinister version of childhood nightmares was entirely another. Taking another sip of my tequila, I drew my arm from her grasp, and shook off the threads of damaged soul light.

The human was right.

Dammit.

From the peripheral of my vision, someone caught my eye. Shaded by palm trees, the tiki hut bar sat past Lilith to her right. I recognized my ever-annoying human sitting in one of the high back chairs with her back turned to us.

Ash.

Dammit. I told her to stay away. I should have realized she wouldn't listen. I guzzled the remainder of my melted margarita.

"Another?" I asked Lilith, pointing to her glass.

"Oh, Ren, they will bring you one." Her words faded behind me as I casually made my way to the front of the bar, and slid my glass to the bartender.

"Margarita, please." I said to the bartender. Wasteful, as demons were unable to become intoxicated, but the flavor of high-end tequila satisfied in other ways.

"Ash." My tone a patronizing whisper. "I told you to let me handle her." She eyed me under reflective sunglasses.

"You felt it, didn't you?" She sipped a strawberry daiquiri from a plastic black straw.

"Straws kill sea turtles, you know."

"A demon with a conscience? How extraordinary." Slurping gurgled from the bottom of the cup.

"You need to go," I said in response to the slurps. The bartender pushed my refill towards me. "Now."

"Yeah, I don't think so, friend." Ash's foot bounced in uneven flutters.

Magic wafted from her.

Huffing out my breath, I settled on the fact she would not leave.

Pulling the straw from the empty glass, Ash smirked, chewing on the end of the plastic.

"Stay," I snapped at her.

As I turned to leave, she muttered something about not being a dog. Humans were impossible, stubborn, fickle creatures. On my short walk back to the doctor I invoked worship she didn't view the exchange.

"Who is she? A possible recruit to our little project?" Lilith glanced back toward the tiki bar, eyeing Ash with curiosity as I sat down.

So much for hope and prayers.

"Ha. Not even close. Minimal soul light, that one." I crossed my legs and gazed at the ocean in disinterest. "Karen, on the other hand." I allowed a smile to creep across my mouth. "Her on-again boyfriend is soon to be off when she finds the secret dating account on his phone. She is currently riding the high vibration of love and will soon crash to an impossible low."

"The sheer pleasure I receive from watching the tumble should be punishable by the Torment Demons." Lilith's hand moved over her chest to contain her laughter. "But I would enjoy that too."

I forced a smile and internally questioned how I didn't see her obviously questionable, sadistic personality flaws before now.

"However, I have another reason for asking you here today," Lilith's sunglasses dipped down her trim nose, gaze meeting mine. "An invitation of sorts."

"Hmm?" My reply was casual as I relaxed back in the chair, interlacing my fingertips behind my head. Immediately sensing Ash's reaction to my casual and overt comfort with Lilith, I realized I would need to do something about her.

"Well, Crastin and I are doing a little more than you are aware of."

"Oh? Do tell me more." I turned my body toward her, pulling into the table, persuasion powers seeping between us.

"If you are to be involved…" She nudged the

sunglasses to the top of her head. "There are certain requirements."

Behind Lilith, Ash made faces at me. Narrowed, puckered, angry faces.

"I would need your absolute discretion and compliance, but the reward, Ren..." Her body leaned into the table, eyes sparking with malevolence, enticing me forward. "The reward is divine."

Divine.

I couldn't decide if I was amused or disgusted by the word she chose to describe decimating human souls as she tried to charm me into her abominable plan. Regardless, with my synergy power blazing, I permitted amusement, interest, and intrigue to filter through my body.

My teeth ran over the edge of my bottom lip, seductively drawing her a few inches closer. "Tell me more."

"Have Karen ready, and I promise you the most delectable experience of your existence." Smoky enthusiasm radiated between us.

My voice lowered to a faint whisper. "Now, that is quite the promise."

Over the left of Lilith's shoulder, Ash slid back her chair with a clamor of wood scraping against cement, apparently losing her patience with me. Magic poured out of her fingertips with one precise target in her sights.

I couldn't let her hurt Lilith. Not now. Not when I was this close to discovering the truth. My mouth twisted and I reacted with quick, precise motion to stop her. I created a mirage between us, and Ash jolted to a stop, eyes fading into confusion. The glamor I forced her to view was a rainy cityscape, and we were safe for the moment.

"When?" The urgency in my voice suited both situations. The time constraint with Ash being held in the glamor and the seductive persuasion I held with Lilith.

"As soon as she is ready." Lilith reached out, squeezing my hand.

Once again, the stinging buzz of human soul energy pulsed through me. I held back from letting my teeth slam together. The intoxicating thrums pulled into me, beckoning my immortality, and I understood her use of the word divine. Unearthly and exotic, I reveled in the delicate flood until the guilt saturated my mind, accompanying the perversion and wickedness I enjoyed.

With force I shook off the enticing waves and the heady cloud of desire, returning my focus back to Lilith, and Ash struggling in the glamor.

"Well, I don't think I can refuse such an offer." The remaining tendrils distracted my attention. Ash may be right, but I needed a better understanding of Lilith's operation before allowing Ash to destroy the doctor.

"I promise I will not disappoint. That was only a taste." Allure rang through her words. "See you soon, Ren."

My muscles trembled at the notion of feeling more.

Lilith sauntered past Ash, still protected within the glamor that made her invisible, to the bar for another drink. My breath released in ragged huffs. In a blink of my eye I disappeared, taking Ash with me.

Prepared for the little human to instantly rip into me with her enraged opinions, I traveled the two of us to her demented hidey-hole. I found the decrepit building depressing, but it was her show, and she seemed to like it here.

"*Why* did you let her escape?" Anger blazing, Ash threw up her arms. "You will not get in my way, demon."

"I didn't allow her to escape, I allowed her to believe I am on her side, like the manipulative persuasive being I am. You should try patience." I folded my hands behind my back. "You are certainly trying *my* patience." I blurted the words under my breath before I could stop them. The building creaked around us as if sensing our discontent. "Perhaps you're not ready for this feat," I said, a little louder.

"Not ready?" Ash snarled, imposing her small presence in bits of flared energy. "I could have killed her easily and ended this!"

"But little lamb, what if you have the wrong wolf?" I asked.

Her anger faltered in the slightest manner as a thought which never occurred to her stumbled into her eyes.

CHAPTER FIVE
Inner Turmoil

Sitting in the dimly lit house, I considered the possibility of needing a new therapist to discuss my current therapist problems. I leaned back in the antique rocking chair and tried to decide if I was actually helping Ash, Lilith, or myself. Therapy didn't feel incredibly helpful at this point, requiring me to constantly reevaluate my choices and decisions. It seemed to only increase my problems, and I wondered why humans bothered. Then again, humans are not the brightest of the bunch. What I should do is go back to my old self and slowly siphon soul light like a normal demonic villain.

I thought about Karen in the next room, her magnificent soul light expanding and waning as she slept. Her warm energy radiated throughout the entire house, touching everything with a delicate devotion. One day humans might recognize they hold all the power, a beautiful essence full of remarkable potential but too oblivious to realize they are capable of destroying us.

Instead both sides, good and evil, have used human energy for millennia to maintain their livelihood. Like a slow draw off a battery, evil used negative impact emotions to siphon energy and the other side used positive emotions, namely *love*, to do the same. The process is identical, except for the choice regarding *how* the energy is claimed.

Although sacrificing Karen's energy to Lilith and her atrocious plan deftly defied my moral compass, the temptation begged me. With that thought, the sensation of human soul energy burst into my mind, taking over my senses. The steady thrum returned as if Lilith touched me again. The flood pushed into the tiniest cracks, invading my consciousness.

An imprint spell. That sly, devious woman. Determined to have me a part of her atrocities, she used magic to ensure my attachment. Newly aware of her work, I searched for the trails of magic and shredded the remainder of the spell. How dare …

Meeeewwwwwllll

Simon's low guttural meow interrupted my thoughts and I met his glowing yellow eyes shimmering in the black void of the hallway.

"Simon. I am not in the mood for our games," I whispered in his direction.

The cat rubbed his body along the door frame before meowing in response. Half begrudgingly, I whipped a trail of light across the room for the orange tabby to chase. Our late-night evening game became customary during the last few months of my time with Karen.

Simon darted around the room, chasing my whips of magic. We had come to an agreement, the cat and I. He gets to be a dick cat and I get to be a dick demon with mutual appreciation for our purpose in life.

Pondering my predicament, I tossed out more flutters of light, the corners of my mouth turning up as the cat jumped in a spiral of movement.

Do I break my rules and take Karen to Lilith?

Suddenly, in a flash of orange, the cat ripped across the floor, paws sliding on the wood as he careened from the room in a scattering ruckus of fear.

Eyebrows furrowing, I wondered what scared the fur-face, and then the rush of cool air sunk into me. Moving in subtle wisps, the fluctuation in energy circled around the room, over the furniture in dips and billows as gooseflesh prickled my skin. Silver beams filtered in and I shifted in the chair, my teeth offset and grinding to one side as my nerves became raw and exposed.

Precious few aspects of my existence were troublesome to me, but dealing with these creatures made it almost intolerable. Each interaction became a more horrific experience than the last.

Time dragged inward, my existence expanding over impossible gaps of moments spun together like an impossible web. The feeling of synchronicity ran in uncomfortable waves, tearing into my body. The ripples fissured, creating tattered edges to my energy, like a bullet ripping through flesh. Then pain began, a feeding frenzy building to a crescendo of horrifying music. I bit down on my tongue, fighting against the violent fire cascading in my veins.

"Renzarmodeus." My full name came out in an abject snarl. The being took form, shifting through many faces, some human, most not. Humans often gave them beautiful human-like faces, but the truth? Their forms were ghastlier than ours.

"To what do I owe this displeasure, Augustine?" I swallowed hard, trying to calm the chaos driving into my bones. Smoothing my robes, I plucked a few Simon hairs from the velvet.

"You have found yourself in quite the debacle." The being quipped with a surly, all-knowing voice. "Engaged in the affairs of those outside your normal domain."

Slithers of discomfort reached out for me, like tiny sharp feathers cutting through my energy. Finally taking full form, he stood, looming above me in an overtly judgmental way, hands hidden in layers of robe.

"Why are you here?" I tried to keep my facial expression neutral.

"You, Karen, the others." In human form now, his head tilted in consideration. "You are on the brink of a life changing decision."

"Life changing? Like what, precisely? I will become one of you?" I spat the words in disgust. Scoffing, I unconsciously recoiled against his presence. "I don't think so."

"Mmm." The sound, short and disbelieving, carried in the silence. Water dripped from the leaky faucet in the hall bathroom. "You play a crucial impact in the events to come."

"Reduced to vague and ambiguous messages, are we?" My eyes narrowed. "Is that why you were sent? To taunt me?"

"We never taunt, Ren." Eyes the color of molten lava bore into mine. "We do forewarn, however. There are things occurring outside of your control."

The insidious piercing of energy wafted through the room again, searching for an entrance to spread despised doctrine in the form of thought patterns and ideas. To find any place to take root and push the boundaries of my beliefs.

Simon peered in from the edge of the doorway, chirping a squabbling meow.

My sentiments as well, Simon.

The orange cat meandered in, as only a cat can do, and jumped on my lap. Sniffing my face, his whiskers tickled my chin before he turned to glare at the ominous being. With a huff he curled into a ball in the folds of my robes and made himself comfortable in a complete invasion of space.

"Let me guess, Ash is working for you imbeciles?" My hands curled around the edges of the chair, the wood cracking with pressure.

"Ah, yes. Ash." The being's eyes glittered. "She is a factor no one considered. A wild card played by Fate."

"Oh, for Heaven's sake. Do not tell me Fate is playing in this fiasco." My head fell back, followed by a rush of grumbling breath. The Fates consisted of multiple entities, controlling different aspects of divine paths. Can't a demon simply meander through its existence without getting involved in the grapplings of destiny?

The being tipped his head with pursed lips, revealing Fate's involvement.

Apparently not.

"If Fate is involved, then why are you?" I glared, meeting the sinister eyes of one of the most repulsive creatures on the planet. "Angels usually take a side seat when such grand plans are being affected."

The nauseating stench of perceived divinity assaulted my senses. As a distraction, the temptation of soft fur became too strong. To stop myself from strangling the angel, I scratched and rubbed Simon's head. A motor of purring began, and he pushed his face into my hand, heedless to the tension surrounding him.

The angel dared to laugh. "As I said, Ren, crucial impact. Our involvement stretches as deep as yours."

The cat's ears twitched, responding to my agitation. This was probably because I interrupted his transcendent state of bliss and not because an angel and demon were close to a skirmish in his human's house.

Once again, the distinct vibration of universal energy poured over me. Angels loved to focus on the interconnectedness of all things, good and evil. Because if evil exists as interconnected as good, then where lies the difference? Only within the perspective of the individual. For a demon, the distinction caused madness and put their existence into question. Hence the pain, the torture, the twists clamoring through my body trying to reject any connection the angel tried to create.

Humans worshiped them and their refined, elaborate manipulation skills. Bleh. The mere thought sickened me.

"Ah, Ren. I believe I have witnessed you complain about these cats, but here you are comforted by them." The angel's eyebrows shot up to make his point, gesturing toward the cat. "In this moment, linked together in love and mutual affection."

"I am petting him," I said through gritted teeth. "Mostly so I don't destroy you, and by default, his home. Do not confuse the matter at hand."

My jaw clenched at the angel's attempt to change the subject, the sordid misdirection blatant. Angels were believed to be virtuous and moral by millions of souls.

If they only knew.

Clueless humans.

"You can take your mind games elsewhere, angel of manipulation." I resumed petting Simon, who forced me to scratch under his chin.

"Remember, I came to forewarn you. There are things at play you know nothing of." In a swooping motion of energy, the angel vanished, leaving trails of opal light dancing in the darkness.

Simon stretched his head upward, yawning with a squeak. The menacing feeling dissipated.

Angels.

My immortal life spanned several thousands of years and I managed to masterfully avoid interactions with the repugnant beings. And now, here I was mixed up in an Altered Course Event. My eyes drifted closed as I sighed. Discontentment with my recent streak of luck blossomed in my chest, gnawing into whatever resolve remained.

The cat decided he accrued enough attention and leapt from my lap, claws sinking into my skin as he went.

Altered Course Event. I had been tagged. Called. Put into play. With absolutely no way out. Once all the players are summoned, Fate holds control and plays its shrewd game of chess, moving pieces until the desired result is reached. These types of events alter the course of history and no one can stop them. They become the paradoxes.

John F Kennedy being shot.

Adolf Hitler.

Discovery of penicillin.

Civil War.

The American Revolution.

The Renaissance.

Christopher Columbus arriving to the Americas.

The Black Death.

The list of events goes on of the moments in history where an outcome changes the future of the world. So now amongst angels, a deadly therapist, and Fate's choice in a five-foot-nothing pain in my ass, I was slated to be involved in the next momentous earth-altering occasion.

Freaking wonderful.

CHAPTER SIX
Friends

The side of my fist tapped the metal square that read "Push to Open" at the internal entrance of the Twin Pines Behavioral Health Clinic and the doors swung open.

"Manny? Did you hit those doors again?" A loud woman's voice called out.

"Nope, JoJo, that ain't me. I told you, those doors are haunted." Manny's deep southern drawl filled the corridor. Two heads popped out of the nurse's station to peer down the long hallway as I drifted by, doors closing behind me.

The Altered Course Event weighing heavily like a bottle of Jack after a bad breakup, I decided I needed a normal day, a day with my friends. Glass walls gave me a clear view of the Rec Room as I searched for Lisa. She had been assigned to me years ago, and we shared a healthy synergetic bond. We collaborated through several of her transformational life events and communicated regularly.

Weaving around a hunched elderly woman quietly working on a mystical forest scene puzzle, I found Lisa sitting on the corner of the depressing gray-blue couch watching the others enjoy their free social time. Plopping down next to her, my robes slid on the weird pleather material.

"Hey Lis." I nudged my arm in her direction.

"You're not real." Lisa stammered in a whisper.

"Is that how you greet a friend?"

"We're not friends. You're not real. They told me you can't be real." Hazy, brown, medicated eyes glazed over me.

"I am real. You know that," I promised in soft, warm tones.

"No. No. I am on meds now. They help me." Lisa's black hair fell in tangles across her face as she rocked forward. She rubbed her hands down her pants, pushing aggressively on her thin legs.

"I've had a rough couple of weeks. You would not believe it! I see a therapist now." I rested my head on the back of the couch, staring up at the speckled gray ceiling tiles.

"No doctors!" Lisa shouted aimlessly to the room.

"Now, Lisa, you calm down and enjoy your free time." The nurse in the corner called out, giving her a warning glare.

"I should have listened to you, Lisa. That would've been helpful weeks ago." My hands dragged over my face. "She is killing humans!"

"You're not real." Lisa chewed on the edge of her thumbnail.

"Lisa! Focus. I need your help. Remember when I helped you?" I asked.

"You didn't help! That's why I am in here!" Lisa's voice pitched higher, gathering more attention.

I groaned. The medications seriously didn't help my cause.

"I am not hurting anyone for you again."

"Hey, now, I never asked you to do that. You decided to shake the baby all on your own," I chided, watching her knee bounce up and down as her agitation increased.

"You did this! You're not real! You. Are. Not. Real!" Lisa stood. The fracture in her mind broke like an ice crevasse on a warm day.

"Oh, Manny, get in here! Lisa, honey, you calm down. It's going to be okay," JoJo said, trying to help as Lisa became more inconsolable.

Seriously? This is the moment she chooses to fall apart? Lisa had always been there for me before. Talk about disappointing.

"Lisa, honey, we're gonna give you a little medication, okay?" The nurse kept her voice quiet and serene as Manny came over to hold Lisa, who was now kicking.

"You know, Lisa, it isn't always about you! I just needed a friend!" The nurses dragged her from the room. Some of the remaining patients became irritated by the disturbance, others didn't notice the commotion.

"'Dem angels used to come and talk to me," a weathered southern drawl called out. From the table next to the couch, a bob of snarly gray hair turned, revealing a tiny old lady holding out a puzzle piece to me. "Dey just as bad as you." Her finger shook as she stared right at me before sliding the piece into the puzzle.

* * *

The confessional window chafed against the wood as it slid open. "Tell me your sins, my son." A gravelly, baritone voice drifted through the grate.

"Thank you, Father." I struggled to sit on the narrow bench. "It has been a long time since my last confession. I barely remember why I came to confess, other than I was on a binge." I shuddered thinking about the first time I confessed to a priest some nine hundred years ago.

"These things can be forgiven, my son."

"Well, Father Joseph, the problem is my therapist." Resting my elbows on my thighs, my head hung as I stared at my feet. "I'm struggling."

"Are you having salacious, or otherwise inappropriate thoughts," the priest asked, understanding rippling through his words.

"What?" I asked. "No. Well, yes, but not for the reasons you're thinking." I folded my arms. "I don't know what to do."

"It's normal to have these kinds of thoughts. You are a man." The Father offered.

"No. No, it is not that," my eyes narrowed at his sexist thinking. "She is killing people, wearing their energies like a damn Edgar suit." Silence encapsulated the small space. "Great movie." I paused, peering through the tiny holes in the window at the flecks of black from the robes of the priest. "Anyway, I feel compelled to stop her."

After a moment the priest finally responded. "I see. Murder is definitely a mortal sin. And…"

I cut him off before he spouted God's word. "Well, right! Precisely my thoughts, too. I mean, I can't allow her to kill humans. It goes against my moral code."

"I am very happy to hear you have a code, my son." Relief filtered in a huff of breath. "Perhaps, you should call the authorities." Concern penetrated the priest's voice.

"Authorities? What? Why would I do that?" I scoffed. "You didn't call the authorities when you hit that biker over on Sunwood Drive. You didn't even slow down!"

Father Joseph stuttered. "What did you say?"

The priest's panic rose in waves. His alarm filled the confessional box, sparking outward in terror.

"That's why I'm here, I thought you would actually help me, without prejudice."

"I'm… I don't know what you are talking about. God would …" He sputtered.

"You didn't seem to have a problem when I suggested you pilfer from the parishioners to obtain the rest of your down payment for the new car, either. I like the red by the way. I mean, I thought you would have chosen soulless black, but the red is nice."

"What? Who are you?" The priest howled through the grates, spittle flying through the little holes.

"I think I remember why my last confession was so long ago. This really is unhelpful," I muttered under my breath and disappeared.

* * *

My ordinary day of demon work morphed into a disaster with every passing second. First, Lisa and her selfish reactions, especially after everything I had done for her. Then Father Joe, I thought for sure he would understand my dilemma. Instead, my usual rounds of visiting friends left me feeling isolated.

My despondent mood led me to wander the streets of St. Louis. The city, illuminated by the lights of downtown, cascaded an orange glow across the sidewalk. Usually, my rounds cheered me up. I wanted to blame the angel. He egged on my temper, but I knew he wasn't the source of my distress. No, the real reason had been prodding me for months, this precipice of an unknown driving at me uncontrollably like a fast-paced train wreck.

"Heyyya buddy. Ya gotta watch where ya goin." A slur of almost indiscernible words fell out of the weaving man's mouth. He ran into me, not the other way around. "Hey, you gots ennie spare change?"

"Chad?" I stuttered, investigating the aged face. It couldn't be. I hadn't seen Chad for well over a year.

"Do I know yous?" The distinctly yellow pallor of his skin, along with the vibrant aroma of alcohol, assaulted me.

"Chad! I thought for sure the Reaper had taken you." My head shook with disbelief. Chad was one of my favorite humans this go around. Although fairly troubled, I thoroughly enjoyed our time together and hated when his abstinence from alcohol interfered with our healthy relationship. He was a unique soul who had access to the other realms and an awareness of angels, demons and magic. His higher dimensional knowledge caused him a lot of problems, but it helped me to understand the human perspective.

"Ha! I dun gone and hide from dat Reaper, multiple times!" A maniacal laughter twisted Chad's face as he gazed up at me. "I ain't seen you for a long time. I thoughts you was a ghost."

"Well, it's been rough, man. You wouldn't believe it." I reached in my robe and pulled out a bottle of Tennessee Whiskey, Chad's favorite. "Here, I brought you something."

Cracking the seal of the bottle, I handed it to Chad. He took a long draw from the bottle swallowing several times before stopping, dribbles of whiskey falling through his yellow-gray beard.

"You come on in my office." He slurred his words together as he turned down an alley.

Finding a seat against the wall of a building next to an unsavory dumpster, he continued to take gulps off the bottle I gave him.

"Man, I missed you, Chad." My head settled against the uneven brick.

"Mmmmhhmmm. Dat's what they all say." Chad chortled, extending his legs, crossing one over the other.

"I bet they do." My arms rested on my knees. "They have me snagged up in an Altered Course Event." I used air quotations to emphasize my frustration.

"You mean like Velcro?" Chad eyed me taking another chug of whiskey.

"Yes! Exactly like Velcro. I knew you understood me, Chad." My smile came naturally. Perhaps today wasn't so bad after all. "Anyway, my therapist is killing humans."

"You seein' a doc? I didn't know they done that sort of thing." Chad's eyebrows furrowed.

"Yeah, something new. I can't say it's super helpful." Relief flooded me, the unburdening of the heaviness fleeing with the comfort of Chad's easy-going nature. The ability humans held to ease one's soul never ceased to surprise me.

"I ain't ever found dem helpful, only makin' more problems." Chad took another swig.

"I thought the *exact* same thing!" Amazing. All my troubles, and Chad understood me and the things I was experiencing.

"You know what you need?" Chad's voice dropped to a whisper as he glanced around. "One of dem hats, made a foil? Keep dem asshat angels outta your bizness."

The laughter erupted from my lips with force. "Yeah, I might need one of those, indeed."

"Seriously, I don't mess 'round with dem. They sneaky and got you doin' things you don't wanna be doin'." Chad's head bobbed in a firm nod before taking another sip. "One of these days, I'll tell you a story when I helped a girl fight an angel." Chad could only look at me with one eye now. The other tightly closed to assist in maintaining his vision focused on one of me, I assumed.

"A girl?" My body swung toward him in a sharp motion. "What girl?"

"Mmmhmm. Tiny little thing." Chad leaned back and his eyes drifted to a close.

"Chad!" I half shouted. "Chad, tell me about the girl. What girl?"

But Chad took a trip to the land of unconsciousness. I prepared myself to touch him before reaching out to shake him, however the results yielded him slumping toward the dumpster in a heap of dead weight.

CHAPTER SEVEN
Point of Perception

I regretted my decision to fervently nurture his addiction. Certainly, Chad had been referring to Ash in his drunken haze. Ash fighting an Angel? I believed it, she appeared angry enough. But what had elicited such an event?

Questions demanding answers swirled in my mind as I searched for Ash. Pulling on the threads of existence, I tugged and followed, looking for her particular energy signature. Since she tended to be quite crafty, using magic to conceal her whereabouts, it tended to blend my frustration and admiration together into a mess of emotions. I questioned her motives and with abruptness I halted my search.

Instead of looking for her, I scoured for her family members, anyone connected to her carrying a similar vibration. Families were generally interconnected by their goals in choosing to do soul work together, leading them to share similarities, which linked them energetically. It should have been easy to find her soul connections, but I found nothing. I flashed through her connection lines again, searching and finding only emptiness.

One of the most practical gifts from my divine source is peering through time, allowing me to trace a human's past to ensure a precise mapping of soul weaknesses. I used it to play into generational emotion patterns, past life trauma, and anything else I found useful. It was a nifty, helpful little tool. I tracked through her energy, linking into her parents, siblings, grandparents, but everything quickly became muddled. The lines I traced disintegrated, leaving me nothing to follow. Irritation bubbled through me. Closing the search, I decided on a more hands-on approach.

There are several planes of existence. Humans exist in one, but access to the others is as simple as shimmering through a doorway. For demons or realm travelers it was akin to traveling to work via the subway or freeway. A transition into a different place. Tired of the blocks and magic Ash always seemed to be using, I decided to approach the source.

I slipped over into the Realm of Memories. A plane where the records of time are kept. All of them. The existence of everything. And everyone. Ash couldn't hide from the Memory Keeper.

I called out to the stacks. "M.K." The Office of Memories appeared as a massive library, expanding a space inconceivable to the human mind. Records stretched on, genealogy, time events, as well as a special section for Altered Course Events, which I should probably visit.

Another time.

My fingers danced along the shiny white marble counter. "M.K!" I shouted, my deep voice extending into the vast rows. Each soul existed as a glimmering ball of light- infinite particles of data stored within the essence of each one.

"Renzar, is that you?" M.K.'s snarky, dramatic tone yelled back from the abyss of organized chaos. "Just a minute, I am coming." An indistinct mumbling could be heard from the Memory Keeper as he sauntered to the desk. A bit wizard-like in appearance, his long beard extended down to his knees. "Renzar, here amongst the dwellers of existence-keeping. My, my. An important, momentous occasion." Sarcasm dripped from his words.

I tried to refrain from rolling my eyes at the incessant troll of a being. "Hilarious."

M.K. glared expectantly, crystal ice blue eyes waiting. The self-righteous little creature needed to grant permission to the viewer. I'd prefer to chuck him down the stacks and watch him tumble.

"I need to view a certain human's lineage."

"I see. And you can't use your normal techniques because…"

How dare he question me? A fire stormed through my chest. Taking a deep breath, my teeth snapped together, grinding as I contemplated my choices. "They obviously did not work." Hardened, precise words edged out.

"Ahhhh… So, the big, bad demon is being blocked. How upsetting." He rested his spindly arms on the counter. "Must be quite the human."

Two could play this game.

"Something you are not." The malice in my tone made my point.

"Well, well, who is it then? I don't have all day." He demanded, face pallid, seemingly unaffected by my direct insult.

"As if day and night play a part in your existence here," I said, folding my arms. "Ash." I slid my bony fingers toward him. Rubbing my fingers against each other resulted in a fine glittery dust being sprinkled into his waiting palm. The most minuscule amount of her essence descended upon the memory keeper and his eyes burst into white mists. Eyeing him with apprehension, I waited as the images shuffled through his mind. But then his eyes sunk into a void of somber darkness. I didn't visit the memory keepers often, however, his reaction wouldn't be deemed ordinary. "M.K.?" I hesitated to touch him.

His face twisted into a morphed vision of horror, and the scream tore out of his mouth in grief-stricken distress. Everything around us vibrated as if experiencing the horror with him. The stacks shifted, swaying into motion, and the essence orbs of humans and magical-kind brightened, screeching against the violence they endured.

Eyes returning to normal, M.K. blinked repeatedly, seeming to try and shake away the images still cascading through him.

"I..." M.K. tried to form words. "I cannot give you the information you seek."

A finality littered his expression. His palm shot up as questions formed in my mind. "If you must know, only the girl can tell you."

Bloody Hell. As if that would happen. A memory keeper who wouldn't spill all the details. Something was definitely amiss.

* * *

A mental ping, like a notification on a cell phone, rattled in my mind. Lilith.

She was ready for Karen.

The time remaining for me to make my decision dwindled by the moment.

As I left the realm of memories, Ash's signature registered on my radar and I slid back into the human realm. Located in the depths of her decrepit building, I observed her from the shadows as she arranged items on an uneven, barely standing folding table.

Precise movements encompassed her as she picked up spelled Chinese fighting stars, twisting them in her fingers. How did she come to possess such violent magical paraphernalia? She snagged a half-eaten burger from its open wrapper, took another vicious bite, chewing with the same focused precision. Shoving her hair behind her ear, she pulled out a bag from underneath the table, and I moved into the room.

"Gahh! Ren. Seriously. Don't scare me like that." Her spine straightened in a jolt of movement.

"Lilith is ready for Karen."

"Good. I am ready for her." She finished chewing. "What are you doing here?" Lips pushing out, she leaned on the table, narrowing her eyes on me.

"May I ask why you're doing this?" I studied Ash as she moved again in a flurry, shoving a notebook in her shoulder bag. Somewhere in a place I didn't dare to explore, I had come to care for her and her safety. Everything about this situation unnerved me, and rarely recognized emotions, like anxiety and worry, trampled into my stomach.

"What?" She didn't bother to glance up, unraveling a piece of material on the table in front of her, revealing a slender dagger.

"What are you doing with that?" Colors reflected off the metal and I could sense the magic from where I stood.

Dragging the cloth over the blade, polishing in small circles, she considered my question. "Why do you care?"

I wanted to ask what drove her to this point and why she was willing to go this far, but the questions caught in my throat, coated with uneasiness.

"Lilith will not be allowed to hurt anyone else." Her hazel eyes ignited with fury.

"If I told you…" I started.

"I don't care, Ren." She held the dagger out in steady stillness. "I don't care what twisted sob story you want to sell. I am doing this."

The determination in her face struck me like a punch to the throat.

The next layer of the Altered Course Event had begun.

CHAPTER EIGHT
Precipice

Legs dangling over the edge of the Park
Avenue building, some thirteen hundred feet in
the sky, I contemplated the concept of death. The
idea swirled, a fleeting notion to my kind.
Although not impossible to kill a demon, it
required an ambitious set of skills. We definitely
couldn't kill ourselves, so we existed as semi-
immortal beings, meandering through decades of
time like a monotonous work week. In moments
like these I tended to hold gratitude for my
invisibility talents, there's nothing like a figure
hanging off the ledge of a building to cause
humans to erupt in a complete lose-their-shit
freak out. Mental health issues as they were, I
didn't blame them.

The precipice of choices elongated before me.

Ash, determined to find Lilith, created an internal, toilsome debate. A part of me yearned to not get involved, aching to revert to my old habits of sipping soul energy like smooth scotch. My prior existence kept me mollified, content to the point of steady normalcy. I didn't ask to be thrust into therapy, certainly not entangled in a moral fiasco, and absolutely not an Altered Course Event.

"Poor you." I recognized in an instant the voice of the Angel of Manipulation. "Melancholy doesn't suit you."

"Fighting humans? Augie, I do believe that violates the rules," I responded. The angel nestled next to me, peering down at the city streets below. Scrutinizing Augustine's close proximity, I wondered about the reason behind his visits, twice within a matter of a week. It created a visible tightness in my jaw.

"Chad has a big mouth." Augustine glanced over with a frown.

"You leave Chad alone," I snipped. A gust of wind tantalized the lengths of our robes.

"Chad can do much better than you." A sneer cascaded the angel's lips.

Narrowing my eyes, I folded my arms, and my weight shifted in a delicate balance on the rim of concrete. "Why are you here, Aug?" My shoulder dropped toward him as I peered down. "And if you want to continue sitting on this perilous edge, you need to tell me what your purpose is with Ash." Tired of being left oblivious and toyed with, like Karen's cats, trickles of annoyance shot up my spine.

"Ah, Ash. You haven't figured her out, hmm?" The smile perpetrating across his mouth made me seriously consider pushing him off the ledge. "Even after your visit to M.K.? Ren, have you lost your touch?" He goaded me as his legs swung in a happy manner.

Angels really pissed me off.

Lips twitching, I raised my fist in the air and in a swift movement, clenched it tightly. Immediately, the harrowing shrieks of angel filled the night air, and glee sprinkled over me as bits of satisfaction spread through my chest in brilliant waves. Surges of low vibrations radiated off Augustine in ripples, akin to sticking human fingers in a light socket, I supposed, subjecting his divine light to shards of oozing despair. The torture didn't last. Demons couldn't keep angels in a negative empath hold for long, but it sure did tickle the heart.

And I enjoyed seeing the hoity-toity light kisser clumsily wrestling with the heavy emotion. Suck evil, *dick*.

"Ren," Augie attempted with exasperated breath. "Was that necessary? I thought we were having a polite conversation."

"Nothing between us is ever polite." I released my fist and Augustine huffed, slumping back with discomfort. "Now, tell me about Ash."

The glint in his eye told me he was less than pleased with my decision to flout my demon talents, not that I cared. He deliberated on what to say. "Fate... is..."

My fist shot up again, ready to fasten the angel in the grips of detrimental emotion if needed. "Do not try to sell me on the angel handbook bullshit line."

"It's not... Renzar, this is more consequential to our existence than you realize. Fate interceded with Ash as..." The angel grappled for words. It was a rare moment to catch an angel unable to articulate. My eyebrows hinged upward in amused concern.

"Ash is here to stir things up, keep us on our toes, right?" I finished for him. Augustine's mouth opened and closed before speaking again.

"Do not reduce her importance to such simplistic words. You sound like a human." He said. "And for the record, I was not trying to fight with her."

"Let me guess, she didn't feel that way about your interaction," I asked, laughter settling in my mouth. The glare I received confirmed my suspicions. Ash didn't appear to trust either side, and with a conviction stronger than most humans. Perhaps the Fate of Altered Course Events, the tricky little entity, knew precisely what he was doing, inciting dissension throughout the existence of all. I had my own few choice words for all the Fates. But, I never particularly liked the Fate who toyed with the paths of innocents, jumbling them into a storm of chaos.

"Look, Augie, I don't really care what Fate intends or doesn't. For that matter, I understand you believe this is some earth-shattering event.

Good luck, I just don't give a ..." My words trailed off as my vision turned black. The angel subjected me to his own variety of torture, searing a fine mist of heavenly light over me. Divine energy cascaded through my crown, causing me to twitch in agitation and discomfort.

Then the images began.

Destruction and devastation crowded into my view, fires erupting across cities, disease and chaos, but the most fearsome image, the one thing which struck terror in my demon existence was the scarcity of humans. A pounding ignited in my chest, and my hands suddenly felt damp against the grainy cement under my grip. Augustine must be overreacting. The alternative left the hairs on my arms zinging with dread.

The city, taking its place again within my field of vision, left a flush of dizziness. Bright red blinking lights of the communication towers located on the rooftops around us seared into my corneas. I blinked away the spots in my eyesight.

"Dramatic much?" I held back my panic as my body continued to process the things he showed me. Sweat trickled down my back as I considered the ramifications.

"This is a possibility." Augustine snipped.

"Of course it is, along with ten million others," I said, still trying to regain my composure.

The angel and demon world endured while in the perilous hands of humans, reliant upon their energy to survive. It was a delicate balance both sides strived to keep steady. If human numbers declined significantly, our world would instantaneously be sent into a tailspin of strife. That's not particularly something I cared to experience. Ever. Fear mongering angels tended to obsess with the likelihood of such things far more than levelheaded demons, which I found highly annoying. It made it difficult to believe him.

"This is different." An insistence in his voice edged into my nerves, penetrating deeply rooted survival instincts. I pushed the intrusive thoughts back.

"It always is, Augie." My head shook, shaking off the flood of heat rushing through my muscles. "Now, tell me about Ash." I asked for the third and final time.

Augustine groaned. "I was trying to convince her to find compassion and forgiveness."

"Ha!" My laugh was immediately drowned out over the harsh roar of a news helicopter trailing past us. "Ash is incapable of either of those things," I said over the thrumming sound of the helicopter blades.

"Every human is capable, if they choose."

"I am not sure what happened to her, but I am willing to guess she is nowhere near that stage of grief."

Demon 101: tampering and extending the cycle of grief. After spending time with Ash, I realized she likely wouldn't be near forgiveness anytime soon. Maybe after killing Lilith.

I stared down at the cars zipping between the buildings, a sea of red lights gleaming against the black roads. "Her sole course of action is to seek revenge upon those who caused her pain."

"Revenge destroys the light of the heart." Anguish rushed through the angel's words. "No wonder you chose to help her."

"That... is not..." But, if I took a moment to be honest with myself, I needed to ask - what was my reason for helping her? My own energetic benefit? Intrusive thoughts stampeded down a dangerous road in my mind, drudging up a mirage of uncomfortable feelings. "Stop." I demanded upon the angel.

"What?" He asked.

"Go find someone else to pull your angel bullshit on." Sensing the tethers he wrapped around my essence, I flicked ribbons of dark energy at his efforts.

"I am only allowing you to see the ramifications of your choices."

"No, you are manipulating my emotions."

"Because I am making you feel?" He gazed my direction. "Hardly, Ren."

Angels infuriated me. They probed your mind, pressing in on all your doubts, creating an intense desire to delve into the purpose of all things, believing everything held divine meaning. Complete and utter rubbish. I didn't have time for his nonsense. The remnants of his divine voodoo persisted at the edges of my thoughts. The ruffled unfurling of angel wings surged in the night air. Augustine disappeared, leaving me with my oppressive thoughts and the decisions I found myself stalling to make.

CHAPTER NINE
Consequences

Intertwining myself amongst the humans soothed the daggers of anger prodding me after my visit with Augustine. He managed to rattle certain emotions, exposing things I didn't care to entertain. I needed to immerse myself in the fluctuations of human energy before I did something I regretted. The excited energy of people relishing in the upcoming weekend surged around me, feeling like an ice-cold beer on a hot summer day.

In my shadowed form I floated through the busy streets of Manhattan. Despite the late hour, the city bustled with those seeking pleasure in the form of close human interaction. People billowed in and out of the bars and clubs, grabbing taxis and Ryde's, while enjoying the Friday night freedom. The thought of Monday morning was a distant glimmer beyond the two full days of escape from their monotonous lives.

My favorite moment.

Excitement traced over their skin, the need to feel alive and sever the dull reality of their week pushed into me, and I lapped the energy, allowing it to mollify the edginess sitting in my bones. I could breathe again.

Sliding into the front seat of the two-year-old sedan, I gathered my inky robes into my lap before peering at Brandon, the Ryde driver. He couldn't see me, of course, but I enjoyed taking rides, intercepting the intense energies leaching off the souls who hopped in and out of the car. The rear passenger door swung open and two guys accompanied by a girl slid into the back seat in a fit of chaotic laughter and chatter.

"Are we ready to hit the next bar," the driver asked, glancing in the rearview mirror at his passengers. I turned in my seat, assessing my new prey. A chorus of yeses and woots filled the sedan. The driver flicked his blinker on and pulled into traffic. "You guys celebrating anything special tonight?"

"Sure are," the girl answered in a Midwest accent. "These two are getting married next week!"

The two guys grinned like foolish teenagers and more screeches bombarded the compact space. Out of town prey. Even better.

"Hey, it sure smells like whiskey in here. Have you been drinking Mr. Ryde Driver?" The blond-haired guy asked. "Amy, don't you smell booze?"

Amy sniffed the air in an exaggerated manner. "Maybe it's us!" Her declaration caused another spasm of snickers.

"Nah, it's probably the poor schlup who was in here last," the fiancé replied. I narrowed my focus on him. He appeared apprehensive about their quick ride share.

The driver, already agitated by his patrons, held up a coin. "Been sober for two years." He wafted the sobriety coin before tossing it back in the cup holder and muttering under his breath.

Brandon's vibrating stream of energy had drawn me into his car. I had followed him for several hours, trailing his building irritability like a mosquito to fresh blood.

Brandon picked up two extra Ryde shifts this weekend to fill his empty nights, avoiding his deserted apartment. His wife left him on Monday during a yelling and screaming blowout which concerned the neighbors in the apartment next door. The reality settled upon him. She was not going to return. I observed Brandon's hands tighten their grip on the steering wheel as the raucous giggling continued from the back seat.

I sent a thought into his mind. *You never have any fun anymore, do you Bran?*

Brandon's mind drove into reactive mode, the spiral of mental gremlins taking control as he flipped the blinker, moving the vehicle over a lane.

Your wife barely wants anything to do with you. It's always about the baby. What about you? You have needs too.

A heaviness impregnated the sedan, unnoticed by the passengers, unraveling the compressed energy of resentment. Fingers flexing on the wheel, Brandon cursed under his breath as a Mercedes cut over in front of him.

She left you, abandoned you, while you tried to maintain two jobs. Two! I sent as the radio belted out the latest song from *Imagine Dragons*.

"You guys can't smell that? I swear it's whiskey." The blond guy looked around the car for the source.

I turned, head cocked, observing the passenger with narrowed eyes.

He's aware of my presence.

The human didn't realize what supernatural gifts he had, nor the sense to use them properly. More humans were becoming enlightened, awakening the collective consciousness within them, repressed after centuries of time. He didn't understand the distinct scent of whiskey was like an essence signature of my presence, wafting around the vehicle. Blondie leaned forward in the seatbelt, invading the driver's space. "Are you sure you're not drinking?"

"Leave him alone, Mike!" His partner pulled him back in the seat.

You do all of this for them. For your wife. For the baby. Put up with drunk assholes, for them.

Brandon slammed on the brakes, stopping at a red light. Three heads jolted forward and back with the abrupt halt of motion. The GPS flashed the destination: one point five miles ahead.

"Hey, buddy, take it easy on the brakes, huh?" Mike adjusted the seatbelt.

"Yeah, sorry about that. We're almost there." Brandon said, grinding out the words in fake pleasantry.

Brandon took a right at the next street, clenching his jaw with the turn. A taxi honked, edging over in front of the sedan, the two bumpers mere inches from each other in a sea of red brake lights. One mile remaining on the GPS, in New York standards, potentially meant another thirty minutes of travel time at this time of night. Blares of horns rang around the Ryde, a crescendo of tension bearing down on Brandon. Everything closing in, his thoughts replicated by the congested traffic, built in his mind.

She left you. With nothing.

The thudding of Brandon's heart consumed my ears as if it were my own, his breathing rapid and erratic as he muttered, jabbing his finger at the phone screen held on a little mount by the media console.

She will never take you back. She went to her mom's, and you know how her mother feels about you.

I didn't have to interject my thoughts anymore. Brandon's mind took over, gremlins engaging in a full onslaught of detrimental thought patterns swept into his darkest fears, and the subtle flow of energy began. I savored every draw, a warmth radiating inward, saturating my bones, washing away all the residual tension pressing in on me. Pleasure blended with relief in a full body satiation, allowing my mind to clear. With each draw I received, Brandon tipped further into the spiral.

Incoherent muttering spilled from the driver, and the passengers in the back exchanged concerned glances.

"Are you okay," Amy asked, reaching her hand to Brandon's shoulder. The touch caused an instant reaction, a frenzy of volatile movement and yelling as he slammed on the gas pedal through the intersection.

Through a red light.

A blur of movement came as I exited the car in a flurry of shadows. I watched the oncoming car slam into the Ryde sedan and the two cars danced in a pirouette through the intersection. Mangled metal ripped apart as the horrid screech of brakes reverberated, slashing the air. The chaos brought a new wave of energy into me, and I lapped it eagerly. People swirled into action, around the two destroyed vehicles, now stationary.

The hiss of a destroyed radiator succumbed to the roar of horns barking into the night. Agitation from other drivers began to compose a symphony of delectable energy driving at the scene of the accident, worry and anger flooding like a tsunami.

I closed my eyes, allowing the sensations to unfurl within me, and a smile permeated my mouth. An unexpected serendipitous misfortune became my revelry, drawing toward me in strands of unseen, radiating power.

Humans shouted as the sirens blared down the street, adding to the glorious song playing before me. Why had I been so worried? Everything would eventually turn out fine, as it always did. Lilith and her dastardly schemes would shift and change. Ash wouldn't *stay* enraged with vengeance, that was the nature of human lifetimes. A reprieve of the burdens recently weighing on me lifted, the lightness becoming euphoric as I continued to absorb the tendrils of pandemonium.

Approaching the two cars, I lingered as Amy hovered over Mike and his husband-to-be. Bleeding scrapes and wounds changed the course of their evening in microseconds. An unconscious Brandon was being checked by another human claiming to be a registered nurse, and I peered through the windshield at the blood coagulating on his temple, seeping down his face in drips of hopelessness. The tender thudding of his heart was slow as shock perused into his body.

Poor Brandon. He would live, of course. I wasn't a monster. These types of events infiltrated into other areas of one's life, and his wife would presumably take him back. Love created bizarre and abnormal reactions in ways I never understood.

The other car, an ancient two-door Chevette, wrecked beyond comprehension, rested in annihilation. Almost unseen, the driver sat slumped in the faded dilapidated seat, face shadowed by the shattered windshield. Something about the shape of the human drew me closer, an irresistible tugging at my subconscious dragged me to peer over the paramedic's shoulder. Hair matted against skin obscured her identity, and trickles of panic jerked into my muscles.

Everything moved in quick, impossible motions, too fast to comprehend. The sirens of the ambulance wailed in my ears as the paramedics pulled her petite frame onto a stretcher. Medical terms being shouted to one another, they moved in synchronized movements as they loaded her into the ambulance. The cervical collar, oxygen mask, and a flurry of human hands blocked my view, suspending the anticipation, confirming what I already expected.

CHAPTER TEN
Repercussions

Understanding filtered into me as the ambulance doors slammed shut, the roar of Manhattan resuming its role as background noise. The delight and alleviation I received from the accident scene crumbled into dust around me, leaving shards of discomfort coursing through my veins. I had done the one thing I never intended.

I caused harm to the only damn being I care about besides myself. Ash.

Internally, I cursed Augustine, contemptuous assumptions rolling into my thoughts. This sort of synchronicity was right up his alley. But, another part of me knew it wasn't just Augustine. It was Fate, the Altered Course Event performing the concerto with precision, abandoning those involved in a whirlwind of chaos. I spared a half glance toward Amy, the couple, and Brandon being loaded into a second ambulance before I disappeared.

I chastised myself for being incredibly obtuse, playing right into the hands of Fate and its expectation that I would fall into my customary demonic habits. By trying to escape my destiny in the Altered Course Event, I only managed to plunge myself deeper. All because a human triggered something inside of me, making me care, forcing me into non-demon characteristics. These mere thoughts produced a decaying pit of revulsion in the bottom of my stomach.

Trailing the ambulance, a thick thread oozing of despair dragged me down the road, mine and Ash's energies tied together in a cacophony of complicated knots.

The emergency room doors opened automatically. The paramedics rushed forward, rolling the gurney into the receiving area. A flurry of nurses and doctors swarmed around as blood pressure, oxygen levels, and injury stats were listed in a battering sequence.

"Ashlynn, can you hear me? Ashlynn?" The

doctor flashed a penlight over her pupils one at a time.

"She's been responsive for the last five minutes or so." The paramedic handed the clipboard to one of the nurses.

"Get this thing off me." Ash tried to yell, but her voice fell flat like a two-pack-a-day smoker.

"We can't remove the cervical collar until we know your neck is okay." A nurse in light blue scrubs tried to reassure, from what I could ascertain, a pissed off Ash.

This was my fault.

"I can freaking feel you, Ren. Did you do this? Did you?" She coughed with force between her biting words, followed by tormented moans. Pain seemed to wash over her, sending her eyes into a flutter. She barely stayed conscious.

"We are going to need to take some x-rays and CT first, before we remove the collar." The doctor said. He rattled to the nurse. "Severe facial lacerations, possible facial fracture, let's get some images. I am also concerned about a possible brain injury or concussion with the confusion. Do we know who Ren is?"

"No, nothing listed here," the nurse replied.

"Ashlynn, you are in the hospital. You've been in an accident. Who is Ren? Someone we can call? Your partner? Parents?"

Ash moaned in response.

The emergency department, recently remodeled, had individual trauma rooms with floor to ceiling glass for viewing and sliding doors for easy access. They moved her into trauma room thirteen and followed examination protocols, hooking up intravenous fluid and offering pain medication before leaving her with the door slightly ajar.

Swooping in through the door, I peered in close, observing the emerging bruises and severe swelling which appeared to worsen by the second. Deep purple spread from under her left eye. Another brash of colorful skin started high on her cheekbone, cascading toward her ear. More bruises took hold around her chin.

"Mmmmm," Ash attempted to speak. "What are you doing here? Go away." Trying to turn her body away from me, she jostled against the intense agony, the cervical collar prohibiting much movement.

A reply stuck in my throat, the unfamiliar feeling of guilt washing into me, trickled by shame. I understood these emotions, I created them regularly in my assignments, leaving humans drowning in unpleasant sensations. However, the discomfort grew inside of me, hammering down and crushing in on my psyche.

"You broke my face," she mumbled, her speech slurring from the mixture of swelling and drugs.

"Maybe you should drive a car from this century." The dilapidated Chevette lacked airbags and I wondered why she drove such a piece of shit car. My nose scrunched as she struggled against the building pain.

"Who are you talking to, honey?" The nurse returned, checking the numbers on the monitor.

"Is she ready?" A male dressed in black scrubs asked from the doorway. The nurse nodded at him.

"Hey Ashlynn, my name is Marc. I'm going to take you down to radiology." He unlocked the brakes on the gurney before maneuvering her toward the door.

"Whatever you say, Marc." Ash gave him a half salute, accompanied by sarcasm as they rolled from the room.

I pushed my presence into the nurse, still in the room, checking her thoughts.

I hope that girl is okay, she has no one. Poor thing. No family to watch over her. Her mind scattered into thoughts of lunch and her other patients, and I withdrew from her energy. A part of my mind trailed, staying with Ash as she descended in the elevator to the basement where radiology was located.

The other half of me, ensnared in the grips of self-loathing, stood frighteningly still. Often, I spent time toying with the ego mind, pulling on the strings of unhealed emotional wounds and ripping the threads of rationality. I developed the process, one of my masterpieces, yet on the inside I felt trapped.

I traveled back to the Ryde fiasco, wishing I could undo and change the event. Alter any minuscule piece of the night to protect Ash, but no matter which way I chose, it ended the same.

"You two are more entangled than I realized."

Augustine appeared behind me in the empty trauma room.

My hand rubbed at the back of my neck before I turned around, eyeing the angel. My lips fired into rapid movement, trying to find words. Tolerance for Augie's visits had officially ended.

"Leave. Now. Before I regret my choices." I growled, anger flooding.

"But don't you already regret them?" The angel tilted his head.

The flare of light saturated the room before I could stop it, and the electricity flickered throughout the emergency department. Machines beeped with errors and codes as the shutter of power expanded, hitting the angel with a jolt.

"Careful, Ren. Lose your temper and you might cause more damage." Augustine rebuked me and filled my mind with images. One image in particular got me. Ash, downstairs in the CT machine as the power flickered. "Don't you think you have done enough?"

Rage boiled underneath my skin and my arm shot out, blasting the angel with lower dimensional energy. The searing attack cascaded into him, orange fiery trails zinging up his arms and over his body, fastening him in a wail of suffering. Exposing him to this level of darkness shattered his higher vibration divinity, and the orange streaks shifted into inky black lines as they traveled upward toward the crown of his head.

I was breaking about a hundred rules and demon codes, but as my fist clenched, forcing the malevolent energy deeper, I realized I was unable to stop. Seconds dragged on as I held him, subjecting him to the heaviness of evil, his light winking in spurts of white underneath the sinister black trails. Without warning, a sudden surge inflated the room, a shimmer appearing as they made their presence known.

More angels.

My hand immediately dropped, my disregard for the rules had been noticed, and the group of angels left with Augustine in tow. Before comprehending my out of control behavior, Ash rolled in with the assistance of her new radiologist buddy.

"Whoa. What happened in here?" Ash asked.

Marc thought she was talking to him. "Huh?" He glanced around. "They must have had a weird power surge, but don't worry, everything is under control." He winked at her.

But Ash eyed me with deep raccoon bruises as she assessed the small room.

"Everything is fine," I said, trying to smooth the quiver of power still seeping from my body.

"The doc will be back in with your results soon. Maybe you can get that collar off." Marc smiled. "Do you want this closed," he asked, holding the sliding glass door.

"Closed. Curtains too, please?" Ash pointed. "The light out there is awful."

"Sure thing." He tugged the curtains before closing the door, giving the illusion of privacy.

"He likes you." I said.

"He does not. He pities me and my broken face." She shimmied her body more upright in the uncomfortable bed. "Now tell me what the hell happened in here."

"Nothing. Don't worry about it." I deflected her questions, but she continued to stare, one puffy eyebrow rising. "I may or may not have choked an angel."

"Is that allowed?"

"Not particularly. But-"

"It was Augustine, that…" Her words broke off into a muttering of curse words.

"I wanted to ask you about him."

"I bet you did." She adjusted the oxygen sensor on her finger. Now it was my turn to stare.

She groaned. "He is an angel, therefore, a douche canoe." She crossed her arms loosely over her abdomen. "He tried to save me. Well, he did save me. But as you know, they always want something in return." Her teeth clenched together.

"Save you?" The pieces started pouring together. The reason behind Ash's determination to kill Lilith. Because she willingly shared the event, my abilities allowed me to see the memories as she experienced them.

The images were disrupted when the doctor slid the door open. *Dammit.*

"Alright, Ashlynn, I have some good news." The doctor paused mid-stride before continuing to her, confusion wrinkling his nose, aware on some subconscious level of my presence. Ash smirked.

"We can take this cervical collar off you."

"Oh, thank God. And it's Ash, not Ashlynn." The doctor removed the foam device. "And the bad news?"

"Well, you do have two facial fractures, but nothing which requires surgery at this point." He pulled a stool over to sit. "One here on your left zygomatic, which is the reason behind all this swelling and bruising. And the other is smaller on your maxilla. You whacked your chin pretty good, which will probably result in some sensitivity in your jaw for a few weeks. I am still waiting on a few more blood tests, just to check. Are there any other areas bothering you, now the initial shock has worn off?" He palpated around her face and neck, fingers poking her collar bone and shoulder joints.

"Not really." Ash winced under his touch.

"Well, barring anything concerning in your blood, I should be able to get you home today." He gazed at the clock, noting the four-a.m. hour. "Do you have someone who can come get you?"

"No." Ash's voice turned hard.

"A friend, anyone?" The doctor's mouth

turned downward. "We need to release you knowing there is someone to help you home."

"Fine. I will find someone." Her head fell back on the bed and her eyes instantly tightened with pain.

He nodded. "The nurse will come in shortly to check on you. And I will be back later with release papers and instructions." He held her gaze, hesitant to leave. He stood, eventually, pushing the stool to the corner before slipping out the door.

An uncomfortable quietness stagnated between us and I almost missed Ash wiping away traces of tears from the corner of her eyes. "What?" She snapped at me.

"I can take you home." I said.

"I think he meant a human, Ren." She wiped her finger at the corner of her eyes before closing them.

"I can take a corporeal form, for a short time." My voice was soft. The words tumbled out, a desperate need to rectify the course I caused.

Ash opened one eye, deciding. "Fine." Her eye fluttered shut again. "Freaking dandy. A demon is taking me home."

CHAPTER ELEVEN
Paths Less Traveled

Corporeal form by possession required an extensive amount of effort and most demons, or angels, for that matter, chose not to bother because of how debilitating it tended to be on our energy. The offering had been instinctual, an almost guttural response in trying to rectify the situation born from residual guilt and shame.

Experiencing these emotions from inside my own body instead of creating them in someone else produced more discomfort than I imagined possible. I chose instead to ignore the building tension and focused instead on creating a human form. Humans were quite adept at ignoring their problems, so I thought I would give it a try.

Perhaps therapy did work.

With my supernatural sight I scanned the area, searching to find a quiet part of the hospital. Sudden apparition generally caused problems. A stall in the men's room not too far down the hall from Ash's room took form in my mind. Concentrating, I imagined the body I wanted to use and with a loud popping noise I appeared in the empty stall.

An uneven breath burst from my mouth as I accustomed myself to the new body, unpleasant zinging running through me as the electrical pulses from my new nervous system established themselves, neurons firing in my brain. The human form was restrictive and confining to the ethereal body. My muscles twitched and contorted before I opened the stall door.

The mirror caught my attention as I entered the larger area. I paused, gazing at my reflection. *This will do just fine.* I ruffled my short, dark hair. Before walking out the door, I materialized a bag for Ash. She would need clothes as most of hers had been marred by the accident, paramedics, and hospital staff.

A steady short knock on the glass jolted Ash from her nap. She sat up in a quick motion, studying my new form with caution. Adjusting the blankets and her gown, she moved with a nervousness I never detected previously. I peered down at my black scrubs before speaking.

"It's me, Ash." I said.

Face twisting, Ash registered my presence within the body standing in front of her.

"Ren? You stole the radiologist's body? No!" Her voice dropped to a whisper-scream. "Ren! Put him back, or get out of his body! What are you doing?" Her eyes became frantic pin balls dancing around the room.

"But..." Confusion brushed through me, the emotions of Marc the radiologist biting into my consciousness.

"You can't take his form! I will find someone else to take me home. Just go!" She sat forward in the bed, emphasizing her point.

"Okay, I understand." I made a mistake, more than I realized, and not just with the choice of body. In my haste, I forgot one major detail in taking a corporeal form - adapting to the emotional mind included with a body. The last time I had taken a human form was some five hundred years ago. The brain suppresses traumatic events, so I forgot the awful parts. Without hesitation, those parts rammed into me. I misjudged Marc-the-radiologist and his uncontrollable hormones.

"I will return," I promised before disappearing.

Quickly jumping forms, I returned the radiologist body and found another. A male named Jason was visiting a friend after heart surgery. He was a much better choice, unrecognizable to anyone in the emergency department, or Ash. I slipped in through her door, glancing up with questioning eyes.

"Is this better," I asked.

Ash spent a moment of intense investigation scouring the new body. The blond hair, green eyes, and what I believed a fairly attractive face for a human, eventually gained approval when she nodded.

"I brought you something." I grabbed a shirt out of the bag before tossing the garment at her.

The black material landed in her hands as she unfurled the t-shirt. The text printed on the front, *Save the Turtles, Skip the Straws* wrapped around a picture of a cute turtle. It made her smirk, or almost smirk. The swelling seemed to seize her entire face, her lips twisting into a wince.

"You're weird." She retrieved a bag of ice from her lap and covered the left side of her face.

"I told you, it's a very real problem." A small smile filled my mouth. "There are other things in there, since your clothes…" I shoved the bag in her lap.

With hesitation she peered at the jeans and shoes before setting it aside. "Thanks."

"Sure."

An awkwardness spread into the room, caressing the corners of the walls. "They said I would be out of here soon. The nurse will be right back." Ash tugged at the blankets again.

"I guess I should have waited." I glanced around the room, eyeballing the stool the doctor slid to the corner an hour prior. The idea of sitting on the bed brought a wave of indigestible emotions. With uneasiness surging across my chest, I rocked back on my heels.

Hormones could surge in an instant, requiring me to adjust my thoughts and reactions. Demons never dealt with such things, so responding to influxes of random emotions tested my patience.

My heart rate kicked up a notch as I struggled to contain the strange assimilation of feelings coursing in my mind. The biological reminders of why corporeal form tended to be disregarded hammered into me, I tried to take a breath and decided on the stool after all.

Finally, the nurse slid the door open, interrupting the uncomfortable silence. "Oh, who do we have here?" The nurse smiled before turning to the computer in the room.

"This is…"

"Ren, I'm…" Our words overlapped each other.

"Nice to meet you." She gazed over her shoulder. "Ash, how's the pain?"

"It's worse. The ice helps, though. I feel like I got hit in the face with a car." The bitterness in her words sunk into the human feelers lurching inside Jason's mind, pressing guilt to the surface. Another reminder of why I didn't like to possess humans.

"Well, let's get you another round of pain medication." The nurse tapped at the keys, before checking Ash's IV.

"So, Ren? You will be taking Ash home?" She

adjusted the drip speed. "The doctor wants you to finish this bag before you leave."

Ash nodded at her.

"Yes. I will be taking care of her." My words sounded formal and stiff. The toes of my shoes bounced on the linoleum as I tried to act normal.

"He's cute." The nurse whispered with a wink. Ash forced a smile. If the nurse knew I was a demon strolling around in a human body, she might change her mind.

"Alright, I will have the doctor sign those release papers and care instructions." She slid the door closed behind her.

My eyes traced a line from the floor to Ash, meeting her gaze. The hazel-blue of her irises softened. She tried to transform, shift into her normal hard-ass exterior, but the memories of her past, the trickles of what she showed me, sat between us. Debating on what to tell me, she moved the bag of ice in her lap. I became aware she was uneasy with the idea of feeling exposed and weak before me.

"It was Christmas Eve, two years ago." She rolled the seam of the ice bag between her fingers, refusing to meet my eyes. "I was late."

Her bottom lip twisted under her teeth as the memories began playing in her mind. Snow accumulated on the sidewalks as Ash bobbled an armful of presents and gift bags as she closed the door of her car. She swore as one of the presents toppled into the wet slush. Reaching to pick it up, her hair fell across her face. She glanced up at her parents' house. She didn't notice it but peering through her memory, I did. The darkness surrounded the house, unfurling in waves of black, hiding the evil inside.

"We always celebrated Christmas Eve night together, opening presents with hot chocolate and cookies. Then we watched our favorite Christmas movies. My brother was supposed to pick the movie." Her despondent tone pulled me from her memories. "I had gotten stuck in traffic because of the snow and was over an hour late." A slight quivering set into her mouth and the color seemed to fade from her face.

Tingles shot down my spine, gooseflesh following in a wave across Jason's skin as I saw Ash open the door to her parents' house. A distinct energy pattern pierced me. Jason recoiled within his trapped consciousness, balking at the sensations unfolding within his body, as his soul fought against mine. He didn't appreciate being subjected to her memories or the heinous potency they held. Human evil inspired by the darkness of many demons and lower level beings left a distinct signature. However, the undertones circling around the house were not of the earth realm or human variety. A vile malevolence stirred, belonging only to the depths of Hell.

"I could smell the blood the second I opened the door. The presents fell out of my arms, I could just sense the ... wrongness." Tears pricked the corners of Ash's eyes. "Then, their screams."

Tears plummeted down her cheeks, soft streams as the horrid wailing replayed in her mind. "I will never forget my mother's screams."

High pitched, guttural cries filled my mind. A vision of the kitchen formed through Ash's memory, her feeling of almost floating movement into the living room as the scene unfolded around her. Her parents, held by tethers of evil and magic, were pinned against a navy-blue wall, hovering several feet above the floor. In the center of the room, her little brother was held suspended in mid-air, surrounded by Torment Demons.

"My brother was supposed to turn eleven the next month," the sob caught in her throat. "These monsters," Ash's eyes pierced mine with sickened hatred, "were *eating him.*" The words were but a whisper. Her jaw trembled.

They weren't eating. Torment demons didn't *eat*. They savagely consumed. Tearing through bone and tissue with a mouth of snarled teeth, a human became a mass of decimated remnants in mere minutes. Ash didn't simply see her brother murdered, she witnessed one of the most horrific sights a human could experience. Something which usually broke the human spirit, rendering them comatose or worse. Blinking out of the memory, I narrowed on Ash.

How did she survive such atrocities?

Torments existed in the darkest realms, their purpose served to torture and consume the vilest of energies. Exposing a Torment Demon to the earth realm, much less the innocent delicacy of human light violated every law of our kind.

I dipped myself back into her memories. Upon seeing Ash enter the room, one of the three

Torments immediately noticed her presence, rapidly turning to face her. Strands of her brother's sinewy muscle hung from its snaggletooth incisors, and a raspy growl escaped its gaping mouth. Blood pooled in dribbles beneath its grotesque form. The sound emanating from Ash became otherworldly, and her mother bellowed, demanding she run.

Panicked fear encapsulated Ash, locking her in place. From my perspective in the memories, I agreed. The smartest most logical choice would have been to run. Escape as fast as possible, because everything in the house would soon be consumed by an evil inconceivable to most humans.

But Ash didn't have my knowledge and the memory continued. The demons bounced on their disjointed, animal-like legs, salivating over their next meal. A fourth figure whirled around veiled by an inky black velvet cloak.

"Oh, we have another guest!"

I recognized the voice instantly.

CHAPTER TWELVE
Truth Revealed

Slender fingers pulled back the velvet material, revealing the familiar blond hair of my therapist. Although I expected Lilith, the knowledge of her involvement obvious, a shard of outrage sent a shockwave jolting me from the memory.

"She," I started.

"Is an evil, psycho, soul-sucking bitch?" Ash finished for me.

As the memories slid back into play I saw Lilith's lips curl, smiling at Ash. Swerving around the Torments and the hanging remnants of Ash's brother, Lilith's gaze caressed Ash with curious scrutiny. The snaggletooth demons bobbed in place behind Lilith, a repulsive gurgling emanating as they sloshed in the tissue and blood underneath their feet.

"This is a lovely surprise." Lilith's fingernail dragged across Ash's cheek. "You've given me a wonderful idea."

The terror boiling in Ash's heart fastened her in place. The thudding of her heart pounded in her ears like a rush of impending deadly waves. She was unable to shift her gaze from her brother's corpse dangling in mid-air, and the horrifying creatures responsible for his death. Her mother's screams became deafening background noise to her brain trying to comprehend everything before her. But like misfiring neurons, she felt caught in a terrifying nightmare, unable to move.

"Do you like my friends? They aren't supposed to be up here." She winked. "But I am a rule breaker." Lilith's eyes sparked, a disturbing lunacy radiating through the room. "You see, I am doing an experiment." Lilith's hand gestured back towards Ash's parents, still pinned against the wall. "I'm trying to figure out what creates the brightest energy signature from humans. Most demons slowly draw energy from you, sucking over long periods of time. I have found these brilliant surges from horrific trauma are absolutely delicious, the consumption much more divine." Lilith's hand stretched toward her, muscle stretching under pale skin. "Like a parent watching…"

"You are evil!" Ash shouted, her voice catching from the gut-wrenching horror bubbling up from her core.

"Depends on the perspective, darling." She smiled. "I am merely surviving."

Lilith circled around the Torments while keeping her gaze on Ash. "We all have basic needs. Humans *need* food and water, I *need* human energy. This has happened for millennia."

Ash's mouth open and closed in a delayed motion, processing the inconceivable wickedness streaming from the woman in front of her. The scene continued to flash through my mind, the Torments gathering around Ash's parents, the screams, the unwavering stillness of Ash's body as she watched the atrocity uncoil, and the slow fracture of her mind pouring out in pieces.

For a moment, I forgot I inhabited a possessed

human body until fragments of Jason's uncomfortable revulsion pierced in steady bites as the strange sensation of blood hammered in my extremities. Balancing this against my own rage of Lilith's use of the Torments became increasingly difficult. Evil, the dark side, demons, all live under a strict code of conduct. Rules can be nudged, manipulated, interpreted to fit the creature using them, but we still maintain the general constructs of our laws.

Allowing the Torments access to human energy could rupture the veil of our shrouded existence. Police or government authorities questioning the extreme nature of a murder scene happened occasionally, however when too much attention was amassed, the higher ups tended to take note.

"She didn't use the Torments earth-side for long." Ash broke the spell of the memory. "For a while she believed the more horrific the trauma the better the energy, but it was too noticeable and was too messy for her." She pushed at the once frozen bag, ice long melted, whooshing back and forth.

"How did…"

"I live? Oh, that's extra special."

The memory pressed into my mind again. Strands of hair sat in front of Ash's eyes, face wet from tears and possibly the splatter of blood from her parents. Voice raw from bone chilling shrieks, Ash begged Lilith to end her life, unfathomable agony consuming her broken mind and heart. The Torments held her arms out wide, splaying her body for what would come, but something halted Lilith. She paused, contemplative, before Ash.

"I have an idea," Lilith said. The Torment demons' eyes widened with enthusiasm, waiting for the command.

"Please, let me die."

"Leave this one alive." Her eyes flickered with excitement. "I want to see what happens. Perhaps this is the key we have been looking for." The devious smile I had come to know well danced across Lilith's mouth.

The survival instinct in Ash shattered hours earlier and the knot of sick dread burning in her belly sunk to a new level of darkness.

Lilith and the Torments disappeared, leaving her heaving on the floor. The remnants of her mother, father, and brother were smears of blood, soaked into the carpet and residual tissue fragments and bits of muscle. Panic rose in spirals, the images replaying as she realized she would now live with her family's deaths every moment of whatever time remained in her life. The mere thought sent another flood of emotion. Ash curled into the fetal position as sobs wracked her body. Time disappeared, minutes melded into hours, as she laid on the floor, until silence triumphed.

"Why didn't she recognize you on the beach?" My question interrupted her spiral into darkness.

Ash eyed me, teeth grabbing her top lip with hesitation.

"Ah," I said, as the reason burst into my mind. She had disguised herself under spells, concealing her soul signature from Lilith in a clever show of furtiveness. Ash continued to surprise me.

Night saturated her parents' house, the wool rug underneath her cheek taking on a new shade of dark as she stared at the dried pool of blood only a foot away.

"Do you want to die?" A voice called out in the

darkness. Fear trampled through her dejected mind, shaken by the presence. A flush of warmth followed, saturating the house. Floaty peacefulness emanated around her body, reaching through the darkness sitting in Ash's heart.

"If you are ready, I will take you." The voice circled around her. "Or, I can help you."

Ash, blindly staring at nothing, barely made a sound, incapable of answering. Her delicate human brain was enveloped in shock as the evil gnawed on her soul light. Torments caused mental derangement with the slightest provocation. I found it amazing that Ash was still conscious.

"You are stronger than most. I can give you your deepest desire."

"Screw you." Ash's voice was almost a whisper.

"Focus on my voice, Ashlynn."

A trail of incandescent silver swirled around her body, a lightness drawing her upward, made her feel like a feather. Her arms fell limply below her torso, as she hung in the air. Tears streamed from the corners of her eyes as she floated in a semi-catatonic state, no longer caring if she survived or not.

"Will you accept the gifts I am able to offer you?" The voice flitted around the room, drifting from ear to ear in hazy loops.

"I…" Feeling betrayed by the comfort surrounding her, she clenched her eyes tight, unsure of how to respond. A ripple of solace trickled in from the angel, a reprieve from the darkness spilling in her mind, and without conscious thought she agreed to the angel's offering.

I knew what would follow as the memory evolved, the graceful touch of celestial energy showering over Ash, the gift of an angel healing. He also changed the evidence of the crime, making it appear as everything it was not, hiding the murders under layers of magic saved for pivotal life-altering occasions.

But as I sifted through the memory, I noticed something peculiar. The air grew soft, Augustine too involved in his healing to notice, but with my demonic time abilities, I whipped back in the memory again. There it was, the distinct alteration chiming indistinctly. But who had been responsible? I searched the trails for the source, however, every time I latched on to the energy it snapped and faded away. Just like when I tried to find Ash. The pattern was identical.

"So, Augustine gave you magic?" My question was intentionally misleading. Ash scrutinized my stolen human body eyes, debating.

"Augustine believes he gave me magic as an accidental byproduct of the complex healing necessary to fix me and my mush brain." She used air quotes to signify Augie's words, exaggerated by an eye roll.

"Do you know who is responsible for the magic?" Under the surface, I was checking her energy for lies and fallacies. I knew the answer before she shook her head. She didn't know. Did Augustine?

"It pisses me off." Ash crossed her arms. "I mean magic is cool shit, I'm not complaining about that, but someone is using me for their own damn agenda."

I would be annoyed too.

"He tried to take it away, to fix what he thought he had done."

Ahh, the fight.

"Alright, Ash, let's get you out of here." The nurse pushed the door open, surprising us both. The last tendrils of memories stirred before evaporating completely.

While Ash went through the process of signing paperwork, I focused my attention on the issue at hand. Magic or not, Ash was still only a human and I would not allow her to be subjected to Lilith's madness again.

As for Lilith, she would suffer for the things she had done. Trickles of fury raced up my arms. My fingers subconsciously tightened, nails digging into my palms, rupturing my tunnel vision, and reminding me of the body I occupied.

Ash chatted with the nurse about her care instructions, her bruised side turned toward me, and guilt stabbed at me. The girl had been through Hell, toyed with by the Fates, and involved in a horror usually only experienced in the movies. A primal need to protect her, to rectify my part in her pain, coursed through my veins as I realized the body I inhabited had a little sister. His emotions mixed with my own, layering the complexity of the situation.

"Yo, Ren!" Ash woohooed as she waved at my blank stare.

I sighed. This body business was distracting. I needed to get out of this hospital and back in my true form.

CHAPTER THIRTEEN
Revenge

After I ditched Jason's body in the nearby men's room, we left the hospital. Jason would be disoriented for a while, but fine overall, after a few hours. I teleported us to Ash's tiny apartment outside of the city. I couldn't bear to take her to the hidden, decrepit hidey-hole building, even though she demanded it. I insisted she take a shower. The acrid smell of expended adrenaline clung to her essence, reminding me of my contribution to the accident. A sharp whine sounded from the shower head as Ash turned on the faucet. My thoughts returned to Lilith.

As if she sensed me, a ping went off in my head.

My next session.

The session I had already delayed once. As a human, Ash would be in a hurry to defeat Lilith because revenge percolated in the darkest, most obsessive ways. Time became this expanding, invincible organism driving rash decisions, which usually led to impulsive mistakes.

For me, because time moved much slower, the need to rush was obsolete. Instead, patience and precise planning for all possible outcomes became my focus. The issue would be convincing Ash to go along with my plan. I knew she would be irritated beyond comprehension that I wouldn't need to hurry.

Humans.

I needed Lilith to believe I was still interested in her scheme. If I missed my therapy session she might question my commitment. Besides, it would allow me the opportunity to search through her energy, digging deeper into the reasons behind her atrocious plans. A nagging irritation rattled in my mind, I needed to understand why she chose to keep Ash alive. I feared the reasons behind her choices.

"My freaking face *hurts.*" Ash opened the bathroom door and I heard the distinct sound of pain reliever bouncing around in a plastic bottle. "My face looks like a bad Pinterest fail with eighties makeup."

"It is pretty hideous." I frowned as she poked her head through the doorway, revealing deep purple bruising around her left orbital bone.

"Uh, thanks, asshole." A scowl accompanied the sarcasm.

"I assume you have a spell for that? Or some type of magic?" Unable to decipher her particular brand of magic, I wondered if she would tell me more about how she used it.

"Not that it's any of your business, demon, but I do." Ash side-eyed me before pulling herself back into the bathroom.

Angels and demons played in the earth realm specifically because of the *lack* of magic. An existence with humans without interference. Magical beings existed on the earth plane, but in hiding, never brandishing their magic for human viewing, and generally stayed out of our way. For Ash to be given magic by an invisible source was outside the context of normal.

"I will need to go to my session with Lilith," I said as an afterthought.

"What?" Her head flew around the door frame again. "Are you kidding me? After everything I showed you?"

The irritation I expected trailed off her in vibrant, red strands of energy. I tried to investigate the origin point.

"She is a terrible therapist!" Ash slammed her hairbrush on the counter.

"But I am still required to see her." I folded my arms, kicking up a foot on the wall behind me. "And if I don't, she will wonder why."

Ash's jaw twitched, offsetting her teeth, annoyance rattling through her. I again focused on the magic radiating off her body. But, like trying to catch a minnow with bare hands, the magic darted out of my grasp. Something about how the magic moved tickled at my subconscious, leaving an unknown, nagging awareness.

* * *

Heavy black clouds saturated the window view of Lilith's downtown Manhattan office, and the stark white couches appearing sulky gray in the uneven shadows of the storm.

"Ren, so glad you could make it." Lilith sat tucked in the corner of the couch. "I was just working on some notes for Karen."

"Looks like rain," I said, searching for the devious wickedness I had seen in Ash's memories. Instead I found relaxed, pale blue eyes.

Lilith turned, gazing out the window. "Yeah, I believe there is a thunderstorm warning."

Grunting a response, I walked to the glass. The stagnant, dense humidity seemed to press in on the thick pane. The impending storm reached out for me, like wisps of fingers ready to take hold.

"How are things going?"

"I've had the unpleasant experience of run-ins with Augie." I crossed my arms, glancing over my shoulder at her.

"Augustine? What does the repugnant, insidious angel want?" She jotted something on the notepad held in her lap.

"Well they are always recruiting." I barked a laugh.

"Ha. Their desperation is amusing." The words sounded forced. Something stirred in her energy, mentioning the angel created visible discomfort.

"How are things going with Karen?" I detected a slight eagerness in her voice as she changed the subject.

I paused, contemplative. "I have other humans I think are more ready." I was curious if she would be as eager to receive other clients, or if she just wanted Karen.

"Mmm." She scribbled something in the margins of the paper. "Any specific reason?" She glanced up at me, feigning disinterest.

"Karen bounces back too quickly. When I think I have her in my grips, she eases out." I lied. The skyline darkened and beads of water streamed down the window.

"We *need* Karen." Her insistence answered my question. "She is an excellent candidate." Lilith tried to smooth the edginess to her voice as she simultaneously ran her hands across the notebook.

"I am curious about your little project." I left the window to sit across from the doctor, sinking into the leather.

Her eyes glittered with excitement. "Oh?"

"Yes. I am wondering how this all started."

"Oh, well, that." She unfolded her leg to tuck the other in its place. "As you know, human energy is a delicacy, but a slow draw is…" Her lips rolled against each other. I raised my eyebrows. "There are those who were trying to find a more impactive punch, so to speak."

"But the slow draw has been used for thousands of years because it is the most effective," I countered.

"Yes, of course, but…" Lilith shifted in the couch again, putting both legs on the floor. "Sometimes we need to make changes for the betterment of our kind."

"Our kind?" An eyebrow shot up, Lilith was not a demon. I did not appreciate her lumping her mutated dark self in with my kind.

"Our side, of course." Her mouth formed a thin line as she corrected herself. "Sometimes things need to change."

"I'm not opposed to change." I said. *Except when you release Torments on innocent humans.* There was a reason the creatures had been banished to the Dark Realms, along with the

Cuddlers, the soul sucking poofs, and the rest. "What kind of *impact* are you referring to?"

Piercing her blue eyes, I hunted for the layers of her deception, searching through the walls and shields, I utilized my demonic gifts in an unkind way.

There.

A hollow abyss of nefarious sludge poured upward from where a soul may have once lived. The moment I exposed the darkness, she became aware that I knew of every single monstrosity she committed and immediately stiffened against the smooth leather. Her spine uncoiled one vertebra at a time, resembling a cobra ready to strike as her head jerked up, affronted by my underhanded exploration.

"You could have asked." The staccato rhythm of her words became sharpened knives.

"You could have told the truth from the beginning." I gave a half shrug of my shoulders.

"Perhaps." She set the notebook and pen aside. "You are a finicky one, Ren. Hard to read. We obviously miscalculated with you." A half laugh bubbled from her lips. "It is apparent you are not ready to embrace the change our kind need to make."

Any response I intended to make was interrupted by the door exploding into tiny pieces of shrapnel. Swirling around, I discovered Ash, a smirk planted on her face and shards of green magic cascading from her fingertips. I had known better than to trust her promise.

"What do we have here?" Ash focused on Lilith.

"Who are you?" Lilith shot up from the sofa. I detected the slightest tremble in her clenched fists when I gazed back at her. "What are you doing here?" Her surprise was quickly disguised by indignation.

"You don't remember me? Killed and tortured so many people, you've lost track?" Ash edged closer, the sizzling green compacting into a ball, her anger driving the magic.

Lilith narrowed her gaze, mind reeling, flying through the possibilities. "You have no idea what you are doing, girl."

"No?" Ash moved around the couch to my right. "I dunno, I kinda think I have the upper hand here, unlike last time." The spiky ball of magic bounced above her palm.

"Do you know her? Ren? Is this your doing?" Lilith dared to give me half a glance.

The edge of my forefinger met my lips covering the smile which came easily. I found it entertaining to watch Lilith caught off guard. "Don't look at me, this is your business."

"You. Decimated. My. Family." Flecks of red burst off Ash in spikes of fluid rage. "You-"

"You're the girl I left alive." Lilith's voice hollowed as a twinge of fear trickled over her face. "I searched everywhere for you. How…"

"How do I have magic? How am I not broken, demented, or locked up?" Enraged fury shivered in Ash's muscles as she slid closer to her target.

Lilith audibly swallowed, peering up from mascaraed lashes. "You knew about her. You led her to me. How could you do this, Ren?" Lilith shifted her focus on me, trying to divert Ash's attention, trying to engage me in her problem.

"She found you on her own. She is very determined." I rested my elbow on the armrest, letting my head sit against my soft fist.

"How dare you turn against your own kind!" Her venom spilled out.

"Me, Lilith!" Ash's fists clenched, ribbons of green emanating in furious waves. "*I* am your problem."

Although, only able to see the side of Ash's no-longer-bruised face, her jaw writhed in wild spasms. Her magic impressive as it looped around Lilith in spirals of crimson, the seething threads nipped into the doctors' body. I tried to determine the current of the magical line. It held a traditional structure I recognized but couldn't place. The mysteriousness of its origin itched in my mind, a fuzzy picture impossible to interpret.

Lilith lifted her chin, narrowing her eyes on me. "You will regret this choice." Her words shook with the vile hatred I had only seen in memories. And in a wave of inky smoke she disappeared.

Huh. I didn't expect that.

"Arrgghhh! Why didn't you tell me she could disappear?"

I shrugged.

"I swear she is slicker than a mob boss in a police interrogation." Ash pushed out her lips with her hands resting on her hips. "I should have just killed her." Ash stalked the perimeter of the office, pausing to glance at the stormy skyline.

Crossing my ankle over my knee, I began to ponder if Ash was actually capable of murder. She'd had several opportunities, but each time allowed me to stop her. Head ticking to the side I thought…

Karen.

Her name became a repetitive constant shouting in my head. Tendrils of broken energy reached out for me. Once a demon connects to an assignment, we can feel the highs and lows of the human, and like a nuclear alarm I sensed Karen's energy plummet, spiraling out of control. Something was wrong. I divided my energy, a piece of me checking on Karen while staying with Ash.

Well. Heaven above.

"We have a slight issue," I said, returning my presence back to the room.

"Hmm?" Ash turned toward me, a crack of lightning bolted across the sky, as if forecasting the imminent problems we had on our hands.

"Karen." I stood. "Lilith went straight to her. I'm assuming to punish me."

Color drained from Ash's face. She recovered quickly, shrugging in her jacket. "Well let's go, where are they?"

Her insistence to sprint headfirst into dangerous situations struck me with compelling fascination. "No. You need to stay here. Karen is my assignment."

"What? Yeah, no way, demon. You're stuck with me." Thinking about how well she listened in the past, I didn't bother to argue. It would only be a waste of time.

CHAPTER FOURTEEN
Fiasco

Appearing in Karen's modest ranch style home, deep in the suburbs of Missouri, we found Lilith magically binding the living room floor. An ancient symbol traced in a solid boundary of black sea salt encircled Lilith and a captive Karen. Dark enchantments and demonic runes swirled in loops of hazy gray around the perimeter. Lilith's use of the old, however, effective method caught me by surprise.

"Ren, Ren, Ren. I thought you were ready. I offered you something extraordinary, an opportunity to change your life and you would rather befriend humans." Lilith stood over Karen, as she finished the ritual.

"Can you believe it, Karen?" Lilith glanced down at a bewildered Karen. "I mean, your demon can't even be bothered."

"I... demon??" Terror bubbled in Karen's eyes.

"He would rather siphon your energy *slowly*." With telekinetic magic of the darker realms, Lilith lifted Karen to a standing position, hovering above the floor. "But I'm not cruel, I want to save you."

Screams of terror escaped Karen as the fastening magic gripped tighter.

"Karen, don't listen to her! She wants to kill you." Ash threw a green ball of energy at Lilith, but it disintegrated upon reaching the circle of magic surrounding them.

"Aww, it's a shame you gave away the one thing you had going for you." Lilith brushed her hands together, releasing the excess salt, eyebrows raising as she continued. "The element of surprise?"

Eyes rolling, Lilith shook her head in annoyance. She circled around the symbol once more, layering the protection magic. Warning signals fired in punches through my body. Demonic power tinged the air, a power Lilith shouldn't have, and in a micro flash I knew what to expect.

Without thinking, I grabbed Ash's body, tucking her behind me as the blast rattled the house, pushing against me in a shockwave of dingy, ashen smoke. Touching Ash brought a new surge of discomfort as her soul light rippled through me.

"Someone has finally caught up." A snide-filled smirk ripped across her mouth.

"Who -"

Lilith cut me off. "There is a lot you don't know, Ren. You chose the wrong side."

With her back to us she raised her hands, finishing the work she began moments ago, calling forth the Torment demons.

Zinging energy balls of magic smashed into the barrier repeatedly as Ash attempted to break the protection spell. Focusing on the element of time, I slowed everything in my mind, Lilith and Ash clamoring for their triumph over one another as Karen's eyes caught my attention.

Cool azure eyes blinked, staring right at me, fear completely absent. In its place, resolute wisdom. A sizzle of light arced through the air, piercing me in the chest, and the spell concealing Karen's identity unraveled. Threads of magic pulsed inside of her, and I realized why Ash's magic seemed so familiar to me. I hadn't been paying attention. Distracted by Ash's memories and Lilith's crazy plan, I missed the similarities.

I allowed Ash access to the ancient magic within her. A voice, graceful and calm, called out in my mind.

Karen, but *not* Karen. Within my demonic time slip I could see *Karen* existed as only a glamor, a spell created to deceive me, and by default, Lilith. A pattern revealed itself, unwinding paths of interlocking pieces all falling into place.

How could I have been so foolish? The soul behind the veil of Karen and her thread of magic was instantly recognizable and a new scale of trepidation seized my body.

The Altered Course Event began with Karen.

Lilith made a critical error.

Yes, Ren, she did. What role do you desire to play?

None. Precious few things troubled Synergy demons, as we followed the exchange of energies, traveling a well-lined path agreed upon by those who formed the standards long ago. I had a list

143

of certain individuals I wished to never encounter. This woman and her coven were at the top.

You are entwined by the will of Fate. You must choose.

Time regained full speed, and in a blur of orange, Simon tore across the room, mewling and clawing at Lilith, breaking the boundary of salt. The cat, who I realized was not actually a cat, ripped through the protection barrier leaving a gaping hole in Lilith's magic. It was a perfect opening for Ash's energy balls, but regrettably, a moment too late. Simon scattered out of the room in a howl of mewls.

From the wide oak floor planks a smear of black billowed up in a viscous cloud. Torment demons took form within the circle. Bony elongated hind legs clawed into the wood as teeth snapped together in ferocious snarls. They focused on their victim. Viewing the creatures via memories did not capture their true vile nature. I had forgotten the stream of foul despair which resonated with their presence. The sound of Ash's heart pounded into my thoughts, escorted by the fear which captured her mind.

Could she handle another encounter with the Torments? I wasn't sure. Although not our typical standard protocol, I entwined Ash within my demonic protective layer of energy. She would be uncomfortable and unhappy with me, but no human should be subjected to the vileness of the Torments twice. Dread seeped over me as I absorbed the fluctuation of negativity wafting from the demons.

"Lilith, you have made a mistake. Call back the demons."

The doctor laughed, uninterested in my warning, and I wondered if the crazed glassy eyes meant she crossed into an unhinged place of insanity.

Renzar, the time has come.

I focused on falling back into the time slip, quick decisions consuming me. Unseen to everyone but me, Karen no longer inhabited her previous physical form. Instead the Triquetra Priestess took shape. The Triquetra witches were a longstanding coven spanning over thousands of years originating from the early Pagan witches. Their singular purpose was to protect humans from us and the existence of authentic magic. If

Ash descended from the Triquetra line, the magic she used now was just a fraction of her power.

Lilith's plan, her existence, was destined for failure.

"Ren! Can't you help!" Ash pulled me from my time lock, magic streaming from her hands, desperate to stop the Torments as they huddled closer to the priestess.

Prepared, because I held Ash in protection, I touched her shoulder with a delicate swoosh. "There are things you don't understand." I tugged her attentive hazel eyes my direction.

Anger flickered. "Ren, don't! I don't want to hear your bullshit right now. I will kill her myself if you won't help." Ash shrugged off my touch, offended by my words.

"No, that…"

Another brash onslaught of negative impact energy drove into my being as Lilith invoked more demonic power. Growls projected from the Torments, two concentrating on the priestess, the other turning toward Ash. Although unable to see her under my protection, the smell of Ash captured its attention.

An elongated snout pushed against the

perimeter of Lilith's circle. Snorting against the salt layer, it searched for an opening, an ebony eye glinting upon finding the break Simon left open. Sinewy taut skin, the color of dried lava, stretched over the demon's body as it came to an abrupt halt. Dipping its head, angular facial bones protruded against the skull as it scraped its irregular, snaggletooth tusk against the runes drawn onto the floor.

Tap. Tap. Tap.

The gruesome creature tapped its bony heel against the wood before lifting snarling lips, revealing razor teeth, the caustic odor of death saturated our noses.

Ash staggered back, outside of my protective energy, instantly assaulted by the pungent presence of evil, and I glided my body in front of the demon.

"You do not belong here." I growled at the beast and in response its teeth snapped in ferocious bites, snipping at the tendrils of my robes. Drawing my hand up, I pulled my fingers back, searing the demon with my powers. It resulted in a yipping howl of ferocious noise. With the snap of my fingers I brought forth a ripple of bright soul light to charge through my hold on the Torment, forcing it to feel the surge. Demons held excess soul light in the place where our souls might have existed, if we had one, and I used it to my advantage. Cringing against my grip, the demon tried to escape, writhing against the magic which held it, and like an imaginary rope of darkness, I circled the chain of enchantment around the beast's throat. With swift movement, the Torment flipped over, detained against the charred wood floor beneath.

I began to chant.

The familiar words of my kind came easily as the incantation rolled in low undulations of old-world Latin, creating the raven-dark mists seeping up from the floor to encompass the Torment. A slow, slithering of energy ribboned around its leathery body, drawing the beast back to the depths of Hell. Shrieks opposing the harsh spell overtook the room, slicing through the air, capturing the attention of Lilith. She didn't particularly like one of her monster babies being sucked back into the dark realm.

"How dare you, Ren!" Lilith whipped around.

The two remaining Torments tracked her movements, vicious teeth exposed.

"Uh oh, buddy. Dr. Soul Sucker and her nasty precious pets are coming for us!" Ash's newfound confidence under my protective energy shined through her eyes. In her hand a mass of swirling red light shimmered.

"I should have killed you when I had the chance."

"Well, you live and learn! Oh, wait!" She fired the bright red ball toward Lilith. "You won't live, bitch." Ash's magic slammed through the protective barrier and nailed Lilith in the shoulder. Burning a white flash of light through the room, the Torments whimpered in response, cringing next to their master.

An alive seed of anger filtered into Ash, feeding her need for revenge. I sensed it too late. Ash wielded another ball, about to battle in ways she wasn't yet prepared for.

Ren you must protect her. The deed shall earn favor with the coven.

A favor with the Triquetra? Uneasiness settled over me. Such things were *never* offered. A cumbersome pressure whooshed through me as I contemplated my choices. I wondered why the witches put Ash in such a predicament in the first place, but they often operated in prophecy, fate, and elaborate divine synchronicity.

Another blast of magic shot into the space, followed by a wave of light. I stepped in front of Ash, terminating the magic in a swoosh of my robes. Abandonment against my own kind would not be received well. Did I need to care about the consequences of my actions? An overwhelming force overtook my mind, an intense desire to rectify the horrors done against Ash. In some obscure level of awareness, I knew the Priestess was responsible for these new-found feelings, as the precipice of her spell pressed in on me like a bone-crushing wave. Allowing the flutter of Triquetra magic to flush through my veins, it enabled me to trace the lineage of the coven, finally locking all the pieces together.

"RENZARMODEUS!" The low throaty voice roared through the room before the presence fully formed before us.

CHAPTER FIFTEEN
Exposed

Coils of ebony shimmers pulled into the center of the room, exposing the being behind the voice. My boss. Not *the* boss, just mine. Crastin. The upper-level demon overseeing my division of Synergy demons and partner in crime to Dr. Cray-cray, was responsible for breaking several magical and demonic ordinances.

Everyone, and the magic spewing everywhere, came to an abrupt stop. Colorful swirls traced the air in precise stillness as he invoked time magic, freezing everything in the room. Ash stood motionless in mid-throw, an electric blue twirl shooting like a starburst while Lilith's mouth stood agape in a silenced shout. Karen hung suspended in mid-air, enveloped in her own concealment spell, combined with Lilith's.

The Torments snarled, snapping their jaws, their saliva hanging in strings, before sitting in front of their master. Shrouded behind the layers of robes obscuring his face, Crastin's long fingers turned open toward the beasts. High pitched whines filled my ears.

"Renzar, this is quite a mess you are involved in." Crastin pushed back the hood of his cloak in a slow whoosh, revealing beady black eyes. The tsk-tsk sound he made mirrored his disappointment. His comfort radiated around his control of the situation and I recognized he didn't know about the involvement of the Triquetra.

"I never understood your obsession with them." Crastin trailed a yellow tainted nail under the surface of Ash's chin as he streamed closer to me. "Humans are but a speck of dust in an hourglass of time."

My lip twitched in annoyance as a revelation rolled over me. I did care about them. I possessed an encompassing desire to feel connected with humans, in my own twisted way. Panic followed. If I cared, what did that mean? Am I less of a demon? A train wreck of thoughts and questions occupied my mind.

I tried to focus on Crastin.

Tendrils of deep black swirled with him as he moved, leaving a smoky trail around time-locked bodies of women. "There are things you don't understand, Renzar. Let Lilith and I handle this situation."

He expected me to walk away. Fire scalded in the pit of my stomach, erupting against his perception of me. My throat burned as I realized he presumed simple obeisance. Explosive surges of fury clutched into my being. I tried to maintain a neutral expression.

"Unless, of course, you would like to reconsider your involvement." Crastin's hand twisted, capturing the attention of the Torments.

The veiled threat forced another slashing of anger. Holding my temper became impossible as the rush of my power streamed in fluid rage, teeming at my fingertips.

To defeat them both, you must use more than negative impact emotion behind your powers. The Priestess's voice shattered inside my head like a live electric wire.

What did she mean?

Their essences have been weakened by taking on shattered human soul light. This fracture creates a hole that is irreparable.

With her statement, I received images in my mind of the dark abyss which sat inside each of them. An orb of sludge swirling, leaking into their being, rooted in the darkness of death.

Using your powers will only feed the vile darkness embedded in their beings.

I silenced the surge of my own anger building in my body, processing the knowledge she offered.

As a Synergy Demon you possess a far greater power, something you have yet to comprehend. This is why you hold a unique connection to humans.

My gaze jumped to Ash, looped in the time magic, seeing beyond her physical appearance to the trails of her magic stemming from a golden cascade of light. Patterns exposed themselves, a connection to Karen, now the priestess, linked together in a geometry of triangles overlapping in circles and bright waves of color. Only seconds of time passed as she showed me the interconnectedness of human magic. Angels and

Demons were focused on taking a portion of their power, not seeing the true potential of the inner magic which connects them together. An awakening blossomed in my chest, hidden truths revealing themselves in rapid succession, and in a wave of my hand I released the time magic holding the room in stillness, opposing Crastin's power.

"Ah, you have changed your mind then." Pride inched Crastin's spine upward and a smile filled his mouth.

"I always align with the triumphant power."

Ash's magic, alive once again, slammed into Lilith, throwing her to the ground and knocking her unconscious as her head bounced on the wood. The heads of the two remaining Torments spun around, focusing their snapping teeth on Ash.

Crastin flicked his hand, motioning the Torments to attack.

Legs springing from the floor, the beasts lunged forward. My hands shot up, fists clenched, and their movement halted. Turning in a slow, confused motion, Ash peered up from her crouched position. In one quick movement, she attacked them with an onslaught of vibrant red energy balls. Magic struck in pulsations against the black flesh of the demon beasts. Crastin roared in response with each direct hit. I threw the Torments against the hard floor in a heap next to the unconscious body of Lilith.

"What are you doing!" Ribbons of death leached across the oak planks as Crastin's anger spread, fanning up the walls in flames of leaden black. Evil engrossed the house. A slithering of darkness rose from the earth below, stabbing in pinpricks against Ash and Karen. The damage created in Crastin's essence became more obvious as I watched him lose control of his magic.

"Crastin, I fear you have made a mistake." The Triquetra Priestess transformed before us, shimmering in flecks of gold. Vibrant twists of emerald green careened around her and wafted through the house, diminishing the horrific undulations of evil. Karen's former body elongated and her mousy brown hair turned a vibrant sable, unfurling in loose curls almost to her waistline. Luscious velvet, indigo in color, hung over her shoulders, her cloak held by a broach of brilliant stones.

"I am Auriella, Priestess of the Triquetra Coven, Keepers of Magic and Ordinances." Her voice carried in glorious waves, piercing Crastin's darkness as he whirled around.

"Tri…" Crastin's voice faded as realization struck. I savored the moment as his eyes flickered, questioning his choices as his dread cut him in tiny slices. No one ever wanted to interfere with the Triquetra.

"Yes, Crastin." She stepped forward as bands of aquamarine pooled in front of her. "You have captured our attention." She edged closer.

Ash stared, trying to comprehend the transformation and sudden shift in energy. "Who? What?"

I circled closer to Ash as she gaped at the Priestess. "What is the Triquetra?" Ash whispered. "Where did Karen go? What is happening?"

I held my finger to my mouth and waited. The Priestess glided toward Crastin, her delicate face expressionless.

"The consequences to your actions will be severe, yet highly appropriate." A delicate eyebrow arched up as slender fingers danced across empty air, weaving a silent spell. Ethereal blue light ribbons reached around Crastin. With no time to respond or react, the blue tendrils tightened. He clenched at his throat, gasping for air. The magic clamped tighter with each gulp of air he tried to take, black swirls of his velvet cloak swaying in havoc. Alabaster white bony fingers clawed at the Priestess's spell and his dark soulless eyes bulged against the pain.

A demonesque part of me tilted in ecstasy, the draw of energy swooping in pleasurable caresses, conflicting with another part of me which twitched with the pain of my own kind.

"Crastin, you have disobeyed your own ordinances, acting against the creed of your kind, breaking the covenant with the Triquetra." Auriella's voice bellowed through the house, a beacon of power and ancient magic. "You know the punishment."

I winced against her words. The Torments would be a lesser sentence than what the priestess would offer. With a mere turn of her hand, the blue light expanded brightly before consuming Crastin.

He disappeared.

"We shall deal with him later." Auriella turned toward Ash and me. Ash gulped, trying to comprehend the sudden disappearance of Crastin. "Ash, I must apologize for the horrors you have experienced, but this was your destined path, leading you to your future with the Triquetra."

Emotions rippled over Ash, the flash of each poignant and prominent as she rolled from awe to anger, processing the entirety of what the witch said. "Are you implying you allowed my parents and brother to be killed by that *monster?*" Ash pointed to the heap of Lilith and Torments. The priestess regarded the pile, frowning.

"Some things cannot be changed." She folded her hands in front of her folds of purple velvet.

"You didn't answer my question!"

"Some events in our lives are catalysts for our destinies."

The sound of Ash's teeth grinding assaulted my ears as she stared at the Priestess, folding her arms.

"She will be adequately punished, if this is what concerns you, my child." Her head tilted to the side.

"No. I mean yes…" Ash twitched, unsure of how to respond. "I…"

"I understand child…"

"Quit calling me child!"

The Priestess' mouth flattened in a firm line. "I apologize. This is difficult, I am sure. But the Triquetra is your home now."

"My home? What? No. I am not going to just be a part of your witchy coven because you say it's part of my destiny!" Ash's irritation bubbled, her eyes widening, beckoning for my interaction.

"The Triquetra is the most powerful faction of magic in existence. Our presence has endured through centuries, holding power against both good and evil. We command their allegiance and compliance for the survival of humans and magic." Her voice heightened as she stepped forward, intimidating even me.

Ash's jaw wavered as she considered the authoritative witch before us, her own potent electricity pulsing forward. I understood Auriella's intentions. Their magic coiled against each other, smears of color expanding in loops of sapphire and fuchsia. The vibration of their power almost inseparable as it developed around us.

Ash would be their future Priestess.

Spellbound by Auriella, and the magic splaying between them and Ash's future, my reaction stuttered. I should have seen it, the tiny micro-movements from the corner of my eye, and I chastised myself as the blast of dark magic flew across the room straight toward Ash. Lilith waited for the perfect moment to take her revenge.

CHAPTER SIXTEEN
Rescue Me

My body flew forward before I managed to create the thought, a guttural response to Ash being in danger. Thick ebony magic slammed into me, twisting in wicked surges of vile black. An emptiness struck me, plunging me into darkness. Heaviness saturated my being, compressing into my bones gnawing on my psyche as sharp agony rippled through me. Floating in an abyss of despondent grief, my thoughts screamed.

Had I failed Ash?

Hanging in a limbo of descending magic, the quelling of light against dark, as Lilith's demonic power shredded in spiral slices, decimated my resolve. She couldn't actually kill me, but devastating annihilation of my essence still caused an enormous amount of pain. Her magic consumed, filling me with a desperation, leaving me unable to separate thoughts from the dismal overwhelming gloom spreading into my body. As Lilith's magic attacked, trying to find any way to destroy, I allowed my mind to fall.

It was my only advantage. Being a Synergy Demon familiar with emotional tides, the fall was akin to a Sunday drive. I searched, a cascade of flowing movement, as the heavy emotions tried to seize my being. I hunted for the tiniest break in the chain, when Lilith's words from our first session rolled through me. *Did you map her soul weaknesses, go through her darkest moments? You must find the precise place to puncture their core and permeate until you create a cesspool of frailty.*

Standard Demon protocol. Her weaknesses, my specialty. Without hesitation, they rolled out before me. Her impulsive reactions and obsession with claiming power, so consuming she didn't bother considering the consequences of involving the Triquetra. I would offer her what she desired most.

My eyes flashed a soulless black as I opened them, once again permitting my Demon influential powers to flow freely. I acknowledged my position on the floor, thrown backward by Lilith's blast of magic.

"Ren!" Ash swooped to my side shaking me at the shoulders. Slight tremors roared through her arms as she considered the inky black swirling in place of my eyes, focused on Lilith. Caught by the shift in my eyes, her body stilled and a smirk was plastered on her face. My body jolted upright, flying toward her in a frightening fashion.

"Oh, you've decided to finally *own* being a demon?" Lilith raised one of her delicately shaped brows. "You are pathetic, created to decimate souls, and you waltz around whining. Poor. You."

I ignored her condescending, flippant remarks and concentrated on her need for power. A bead of human soul light formed at my fingertips. Temptation trickling in a shower of light invited Lilith forward. Mesmerized in a trance of my creation, I beckoned her mind.

I will give you Ash's soul.

Inside Lilith's mind, an infinitesimal fracture began, unable to resist the allure of my offering. The bead of Ash's soul expanded, the brilliant orb shimmering iridescent flecks of light, magnificent pulses of pure life energy.

"Ren!" Ash's voice held concern as I dipped into her soul signature. "What are you doing?"

Perhaps the swirling black of my eyes and borrowing of her energy was troublesome. I could feel the lilt of Ash's corporeal body as I continued to pull.

I hoped she would hang on just a moment longer.

We can defeat the priestess, overtake Ash and rise to power.

I offered Lilith more and her eyes fluttered, awaiting my proposition. Ash shouted again and with a twist of my hand I locked her into a spell. She pounded on an imaginary wall in front of her, intriguing Lilith more.

We can rule the underworld.

At last, with the final piece of coaxing, the fracture elongated, the fissures reaching out in tendrils, oozing from the core of her soul. Energetically, I delved into her mind and ripped, breaking her connection with reality. A harrowing shriek sizzled the air as Lilith clawed at the sides of her head, the agony shooting in ripples. The shattering of a soul was not intended to be felt in the earth realm. Slamming my palms together, I began the spell to send Lilith and the Torments back to the dark realm. Lilith's face twisted in horror as she experienced the fragile rupturing of her conscious mind, the very thing she had done to so many innocent souls. Ash deserved to witness Lilith's demise, so with a turn of my wrist, I released her from the spell.

In a distorted whirl of Torment and Lilith, they spun together in furious whips of magic before disappearing in a cloud of black mist. I locked them in the depths of a containment spell in the Realm of Hidden Shadows. Lilith's destroyed and corrupt essence belonged with those who were doomed to a soulless, partial existence. The murky smear staining the floorboards was all that remained.

"She really was a terrible therapist." My eyes flashed back to their normal appearance. Ash considered me for the briefest moment, stepping backward with hesitation, making sure I was no longer a threat.

"I told you!" Ash leaned forward, hands

resting on her knees, breath sputtering out of her. "I can't believe she's gone."

"She is in the Dark Realm of Hidden Shadows where she belongs." I released my hands, closing the magic. I would deal with her later.

"Well done, Renzar."

Auriella. I had momentarily forgotten about the Priestess.

"The Triquetra holds profound gratitude for saving our future priestess." Auriella's voice cascaded over me.

"Future what?" Ash interrupted, folding her arms. "Oh no, I don't think so lady. I did not agree to anything."

"But you will," Auriella promised.

Ash eyed her, trails of magic still rippling around her. I wondered if she sensed the ancient magic teeming in her bones, awaiting acknowledgment. The moment she claimed her power, owned her light and her place in the magical community, everything in her life would change. An uncomfortable emotion poured over me. I tried to comprehend the wave as it tingled through my being.

Pride.

This mere child, by demon standards, had conquered a depth of horror most wouldn't survive. Humans continued to leave me awestruck by their ability to overcome the impossible, enduring through soul shattering events pressed on them by the Fates.

Auriella disrupted my onslaught of feelings. "And in a manner contradictory to our standards, you shall continue to work with Renzar."

My head jerked. *She would?* I didn't appreciate being told what I would do any more than Ash did. The priestess nodded, a smile breaking her lips, as she considered us both. To her, Ash and I, were similar beyond comprehension.

"Sometimes we must embrace change and be willing to follow new paths to create a better world," Auriella said.

"I doubt any member of the Triquetra would cooperate with a demon." I folded my hands within my robes.

"Ah, but are you truly a demon?" Her question charred my mind, digging into my essence, as her azure eyes pierced mine.

"Wait, I want to know what happened to Karen," Ash demanded, crossing her arms.

"Karen was a glamor, she doesn't exist."

"But..." Ash's brain tried to wrap around a new level of magic.

"I created Karen with the assistance of the Triquetrum stone. Her soul would be assigned to Ren, so the coven could expose Lilith and those working with her. My plan worked with exquisite precision. Invoking the Fate of Altered Course Events, I knew Ren would not fail to meet his destiny."

"Wait..." I stopped Auriella.

The Priestess paused waiting for me to comprehend. She exploited my time magic, playing the last few months from her perspective. The Altered Course Event was devised for me, a Synergy Demon. The unique energetic connection I created and shared with humans, Ash included, would be the key to unlocking my own fate, along with Ash's.

"But how did you know I would save her?" I stuttered as realization sauntered over me. Jumping in front of Lilith's deathly magic, I had saved Ash, thereby preforming my part in the Altered Course event and changing the course of history.

Stepping close, Auriella studied my demonic eyes before speaking. "Because, Renzar, I have seen the future. I have seen your place in it, and Ash's. You are more than you believe."

Another wave of coven magic rushed into me. I wanted to be angry with the Priestess for using me for her own agenda, much like Ash had felt. In some distant place perhaps I was, until she showed me Ash's soul.

Spires of light emanated from her heart, a unique glow which revealed the future she would now have because I saved her. A butterfly effect spiraled outward, reaching an indeterminable number of humans in tethers of illumination, impacting the future in countless ways.

Auriella's question penetrated again.

What kind of demon am I?

EPILOGUE

"Well, Dr Dye, I think that pretty much brings you up to speed. The last few weeks have been…" I huffed out my breath. "A shit show, really. And I feel like I've lost my identity."

I replayed the past day or two in my mind, Ash and I working together with the coven. The thought was still unfathomable and created a sense of uncertainty in me.

The human psychiatrist tried to hide his overwhelming astonishment as he rested the side of his head against his fist, fluffy white hair splaying between his knuckles. "That is quite the wild story."

I waited for him to make notes, refer to the papers which slid off his lap during my speech, and pull out shackles to haul me away. But he only waited.

"Ren, my job isn't to give you advice, or to tell you that you're crazy." He seemed to sense my fragile fears surrounding my previous experiences with therapists. "I just met you. My job is to help you feel better about the things occurring in your life." The doctor rubbed at the leather of the chair.

"I would like to meet again to hear more about this... new career path." The doctor finally settled on the words. "And see if we can work together to create some tools to assist you as you transition through this particular difficulty."

"Really?" My eyes narrowed, expecting ulterior motives to swarm around him. But instead, only ripples of interest and concern emanated in his warm brown eyes.

"Yes, really." His mouth pinched together in a half smile. "Oh, what were those four words I told you earlier?"

"Red, cat, house, ball," I repeated, answering the final question of his mental status exam. I didn't think he would appreciate the fact I could search back through time to find the answers if I needed. He seemed content enough, so it was probably best not to mention those aspects of my abilities. Yet.

"Very good." Dr. Dye shifted in the chair before crossing one leg over the other. "Should we schedule another session?"

I nodded in agreement and we arranged our next session before I left his office. As I closed the door behind me the doctor's thoughts rattled in my mind.

What an interesting case, I wonder why this man believes he's a demon.

ACKNOWLEDGMENTS

First, you. The reader. Thank you. For picking up this book and taking precious moments of your life to spend time in my world. Every child has a dream when they are little, and this is one of mine. So, thank you for being a part of my dream.

This story wouldn't be the same without my Sexy Ditch Chickens. You ladies are my heroes. Without on-the-fly brainstorming, world building, and the kismit moments of hysterics (the good kind) I dunno where I would be. Perhaps, only in a gutter instead of the ditch where I belong. We may never know. Seriously though, I honor each of you and your beautiful soul lights for being authentically YOU every day. There is no amount of words which will express my gratitude for our friendship.

Amy, we will teleport soon enough, laundry basket or not. Thank you for being a constant support for this story. Your encouragement saved me on more than one occasion. Go ahead, put that in your journal.

Andrea, thank you for every second you spent with my words, making them shine brighter than I dreamed possible. You made editing a breeze and I bow to your word wizardry.

Debbie, you gave me the courage to believe in my writing and that perhaps, just maybe, I wasn't delusional. (Okay, I am, but that is another matter entirely.) Remembering where I was a year ago to now, proves magic and miracles are possible.

Bridget, wow. Thank you for coming into my space at the precise moment I needed, for expanding my belief in myself and my dreams. I love when the magic of synchronicity is so loud it is impossible to ignore. Particularly when accompanied by perfectly timed thunder and lightning.

My boys and husband. Your eagerness to hear my stories always inspires me to be and do more. Thank you for listening to all my crazy ideas and plots, for offering your own inspirations, and creating characters with me. Here is to many more road trips with mom's live readings including all the crazy character voices.

About the Author

Finn O'Malley is an elemental goddess who loves writing, crystals and daydreaming about her next meal. She lives in Northern Utah with her human husband, two lovable teenagers, and two cat overlords on the hunt for adventure, world domination, and wet food. When she is not in her garden growing human-sized bushels of herbs, you can find Finn sitting on a mountaintop practicing yoga or penning witty urban fantasy adventures for humans who need a break from reality.

Follow her at:
www.finnomalley.com
www.facebook.com/FinnOMalleyauthor
Instagram @finn.omalley.author

Made in the USA
Middletown, DE
26 April 2022